FERMINA MÁRQUEZ

'FERMINA MÁRQUEZ is set in a boys' school just outside Paris in the 1890s: Roman Catholic and traditional but also cosmopolitan and rather dashing. Fermina herself is a young Colombian beauty who comes to visit her brother, a pupil at the school. The story examines the disturbing effect of her presence there on some of the older boys – in particular on the school swat, who identifies with Julius Caesar and makes a stern resolution to seduce her. As a psychological study of male adolescence it is delicate, touching, unsentimental; the atmosphere of the school is evoked with an unforgettable nostalgic vivacity'

Francis Wyndham

VALERY LARBAUD

Larbaud (1881–1957) was a passionate Anglophile who translated many writers including Samuel Butler, James Joyce and Sir Thomas Browne. In 1935 he suffered a severe stroke which incapacitated him for the remaining twenty-two years of his life.

VALERY LARBAUD

Fermina Márquez

Translated from the French by
HUBERT GIBBS
With an Introduction by
FRANCIS WYNDHAM

QUARTET ENCOUNTERS

Quartet Books   London   New York

First published in English in Great Britain
by Quartet Books Limited 1988
A member of the Namara Group
27/29 Goodge Street, London W1P 1FD

British Library Cataloguing in Publication Data

Larbaud, Valery
 Fermina Márquez.
 I. Title
 843'.912[F]

ISBN 0-7043-0046-7

Typeset by MC Typeset Limited, Chatham, Kent

Printed and bound in Great Britain by
The Camelot Press, plc, Southampton

INTRODUCTION

It is rare for a writer to be born extremely rich. In many cases great
wealth might prove a handicap to the development of a literary gift
but Valery Larbaud (1881–1957) succeeded in turning his financial
assets to artistically creative advantage. The source of his money
was the Saint Yorre mineral spring at Vichy, which he inherited
from his father at the age of eight: it could be said that, throughout
the *belle époque* and the years between the wars, whenever a glass
of Vichy water was drunk anywhere in the world a centime or so
was added to Larbaud's fortune. The image thus evoked is wholly
appropriate, for Larbaud was to become the poet of first-class
travel, exploiting a sensibility perfectly attuned to the melancholy
glamour of sleeping-cars, ocean liners and Ritz hotels.

> I felt all the sweetness of life for the first time in a compartment
> of the Nord express between Wirballen and Pskov. We were
> slipping through grasslands where shepherds, at the foot of
> clumps of big trees like hills, were dressed in dirty, raw
> sheepskins . . .
> Lend me your vast noise, your vast gentle speed, your nightly
> slipping through a lighted Europe, O luxury train! And the
> agonizing music that sounds the length of your gilt corridors,
> while behind the japanned doors with heavy copper latches sleep
> the millionaires . . .

Throughout his childhood and adolescence Larbaud was dominated by his formidable widowed mother, whose vigilance extended into his young manhood and under whose oppressive
chaperonage he voyaged round Europe (but escaping her for long

enough to enjoy discreet love affairs with young women in every country visited) while he wrote poetry, fiction and travel essays. His best-known work, *A.O. Barnabooth*, is a combination of all these genres, describing the spiritual, aesthetic and erotic adventures of a young South American millionaire as he fastidiously journeys along the same privileged, exotic routes that Larbaud had explored for himself. This was published in 1913; still not quite free of Madame Larbaud's influence, he was by then himself an influential figure on the French literary scene, a friend of André Gide and a prominent member of the group of intellectuals associated with the *Nouvelle Revue Française*.

Larbaud was a highly civilized example of everything that is understood by the phrase 'man of letters'. His sympathies, expressed in a vast output of literary criticism (including two collections with the overall tile *Reading – That Unpunished Vice*), were generous and wide. An authority on Hispanic, English and American literature, he translated several Spanish and Portuguese writers into French as well as poems by Coleridge and Walt Whitman, prose by Sir Thomas Browne and Nathaniel Hawthorne, a novel by Arnold Bennett and almost the entire work of Samuel Butler. He also collaborated with James Joyce (and others) on the French version of *Ulysses*.

Larbaud had met Joyce in Paris in 1920 and had been excited by the parts of *Ulysses* that had so far appeared. The following year he published a long story called *Amants, Heureux Amants . . .* which was told as an interior monologue, and acknowledged its influence in the dedication: 'To James Joyce, my friend and the only begetter of the form I have adopted in this piece of writing.' Joyce immediately corrected him, pointing out that the true originator (and his own inspiration) was Edouard Dujardin, whose *Les Lauriers Sont Coupés* had been written as long ago as 1887: Larbaud, believing that he was introducing the stream-of-consciousness technique into French literature, was in fact merely reviving it. He made amends in 1923 by dedicating his next exercise in the genre, *Mon Plus Secret Conseil*, to Dujardin himself.

A passionate Anglophile, Larbaud paid several visits to England between 1907 and 1914, vaguely researching a projected biography of Walter Savage Landor. His lyrical treatment of places which English readers may take rather prosaically for granted can sometimes be a cause of amused delight – in such poems, for example, as 'Madame Tussaud's', 'Matin de Novembre Près d'Abingdon' and 'Londres' ('*Les façades de Scott's, du Criterion, du London Pavilion/Sont éclairées comme par un soleil de l'Océan Indien*') or in the story *Gwenny-Toute-Seule* which is set in Florence Villa, Stafford Road, Weston-super-Mare. In the charming novella *Beauté, Mon Beau Souci*, which takes place for the most part in Chelsea, Queenie the heroine explains that she lives in '*Harlesden. Après Kensal Rise, dans cette direction.*' In her mouth, these names take on for the enamoured hero the melodious magic of enchanted groves . . . The humour here is intentional – Larbaud can be very funny. A group of poems attributed to his *alter ego*, Barnabooth the rich amateur, are subtitled *Les Borborygmes* – stomach rumbles, 'the only human voice that does not lie'.

In 1935, Valery Larbaud suffered a severe heart attack which tragically incapacitated him for the remaining twenty-two years of his life.

Fermina Márquez, his first novel, was published in 1911, when he was thirty. It is set in Saint Augustine's, a boys' school just outside Paris – Roman Catholic and traditional but also cosmopolitan and rather dashing. Fermina herself is a young South American beauty who comes to visit her brother, a pupil at the school. The story examines the disturbing effect of her presence on some of the older boys – in particular on Joanny Léniot, the school swat, who identifies with Julius Caesar and makes a stern resolution to seduce her. But she is more successfully pursued by the handsome, sophisticated Santos Iturria from Monterey.

The model for Saint Augustine's was Sainte-Barbe-des-Champs, at Fontenay-aux-Roses, where Larbaud spent the happiest years of his childhood as a brilliant pupil from 1891 to 1894 – that is to say, between the ages of ten and thirteen. Here the seeds were nurtured of that *cosmopolitisme* which the adult Larbaud, in his life and work, was so fruitfully to epitomize. He put some of his own characteristics (his industry, his timidity, his Roman self-discipline, his pride in scholastic achievement) into the figure of Léniot and others perhaps into that of poor little Camille Moûtier, but Larbaud and his friends at the college were in fact some years younger than the boys described in the novel.

Larbaud in his later books was to write more smoothly than he does in this one, which if judged by the highest standards is not without flaws. The design is somewhat formless, and the spontaneous ardours of post-pubertal emotion are occasionally expressed in a 'poetic' style which only narrowly avoids embarrassing us. But as a psychological study of male adolescence it is on the whole delicate, touching and unsentimental, while the faintly sinister atmosphere of this unusually glamorous school is evoked with a nostalgic vivacity that has proved powerful enough to establish *Fermina Márquez* in France as a minor classic. It seems to me one of those personal, intense, romantic books which, if one responds to them at all, are likely to haunt one with a peculiar poignancy for the rest of one's life.

Francis Wyndham

I

The glint of light from the visiting room's glass door flashed suddenly over the schoolyard's sandy ground to our feet. Santos looked up and said: "Look, girls."

So we all stared at the perron, where two girls dressed in blue as well as a plump lady in black were indeed standing next to the prefect of studies. All four descended the few steps and, following the avenue which bordered the yard, made for the far end of the grounds, for the terrace whence the valley of the Seine could be seen with Paris in the distance. The prefect of studies was showing the new pupil's relations the sights of his school for the first and last time.

As the girls were walking along the large oval yard, where pupils of all classes were assembled, each of us inspected them at his leisure.

We were a set of impudent, sly young men (between the ages of sixteen and nineteen) who staked our honour on daring anything when it came to disobedience and insolence. We were not brought up in the French tradition and besides, we French were very much in the minority at the school; so much so that the language the pupils commonly spoke amongst themselves was Spanish. The institution's prevailing character-istic was the mockery of all squeamishness and the veneration of the most austere virtues. In short, it was a place where you could hear these words uttered with a heroic ring a hundred times a day: "We South Americans."

Those who would say that (Santos and the others) made up an élite from which all the *exotic* pupils (Orientals, Persians, Siamese) were excluded, an élite into which we French were admitted however, in the first place because we were at home in our own country, and then because as a nation we were almost the equals historically of the noble race, the people of reason. That is a feeling we seem to have lost today: you might think we were bastards who were embarrassed to talk about our fathers. These sons of Montevideo shipowners, of guano merchants from Callao, of hat makers from Equador, felt themselves to be the descendants of the Conquistadors to the cores of their being and at every moment of their lives. The respect in which they held Spanish blood – even when this was slightly mixed, as in most cases with them it was, with Indian blood – was so great that all nobiliary pride, all caste fanaticism seem insignificant compared with that sense, the certainty that for ancestors they had peasants who came from Castile or the Asturias. What could be better after all than to live amongst people with such self-respect (and they were scarcely more than children)? I am sure that the small number of former pupils who have stayed in France today gratefully remember our old, illustrious school, Saint Augustine's, more cosmopolitan than a world exhibition, abandoned now, already closed for fifteen years . . .

It was with the memories of one of the most renowned of all nations that we grew up there; Castile was our second country and for years we considered the New World and Spain as being other Holy Lands where God, through the agency of a race of heroes, had put his marvels on display. – Yes, the ethos which had most influence on us was that of the pioneer, of the hero; we did our best to resemble the eldest amongst us whom we admired: Santos for example; his younger brother Pablo; we would innocently copy their behaviour, even the timbre of their voices, and thereby derived great pleasure. This was why we were all standing at this moment near the myrtle hedge which separated the yard from the great avenue in the grounds, overcoming our timidity to gawp at the foreign ladies with unabashed forwardness.

As for the girls, they boldly withstood our combined scrutiny. The older one especially: she walked slowly in front of us, took each one of us in without even once batting an eyelid. When they had gone past, Pablo said very loudly: "pretty girls"; it was what we were all thinking. Then in few words we each gave our verdicts. On the whole, the younger of the two sisters, the one who had a thick coil of black hair running down her back, tied up in a bow with a wide blue ribbon, the little one, was thought beneath our notice or at least too young (she was perhaps twelve or thirteen years old) to merit our attention: we were such men!

But the elder one! We could not find words to express her beauty; or rather, we only hit upon the commonplace which evoked nothing at all; compliments such as velvet eyes, bough in flower, etc, etc. Her sixteen-year-old's waist was so supple and yet so firm; and her hips beneath that waist, might they not be compared to a triumphal garland? And that confident, dancing step showed that this dazzling creature was aware that she adorned the setting in which she was walking . . . Truly, she conjured up a dream of all life's happiness.

"And her shoes, clothes and hairstyle — they're the most recent fashions," was the conclusion of Demoisel, a tall Negro aged eighteen, a brute who habitually claimed, without caring to elaborate further, that his own mother was a "Pahisian from Pahis" and the queen of refined taste in Port-au-Prince.

II

Now we needed precise information; we were certainly not going to sit down by ourselves and probe our innermost feelings like well-behaved little schoolboys. First we had to know who *she* was.

Ortega was the only native Spaniard amongst us and for this reason we treated him with deference. Santos set us the example here as in other things. He was really eager to show the young Castilian that he, Santos Iturria of Monterey, had none, absolutely none, of the vulgar, crude South American parvenu in him. He who dominated our little world through his strength and articulateness, was happy to give precedence to the weak, indolent, taciturn Ortega in not a few matters. So it was that in this affair he asked him his opinion first of all. Ortega observed the life of the school, the small, everyday occurrences, the comings and goings of masters and pupils. He answered that he thought these girls were the sisters of Márquez, a new boy, who had entered the second form not long before. He had guessed correctly.

By twisting his wrist for a long time, Demoisel first wrung from little Márquez the Christian name of his younger sister, Pilar; then by twisting slightly harder, he discovered that the eldest was called Fermina. We were standing there watching this torture scene: the Negro shouting in the child's face, the child looking at him resolutely and saying nothing, tears streaming down his cheeks. Courage of that sort is not in keeping with untruthfulness: Márquez was not deceiving us. So we had a word now, a name to repeat to ourselves under our breath, of all names the one which designated her: Fermina, Ferminita . . . just letters in a certain order, a group of syllables, an object without being and yet containing an image and memories, in short something of *her*: you said this word out loud and if she were there, you could make this beautiful girl turn round. Yes, a name to write in our exercise books, in the margins of the rough copies of our Greek proses so as to come across it there again many years later, and on rediscovering it to recite, solemnly, with heartfelt emotion, the foolish words of a lovesong . . .

"Enough of that brutality; leave him be. Go on, just leave him be!" said Santos to Demoisel. The Negro obeyed grudgingly, whereupon little Márquez, starting to talk freely, told us that the plump lady accompanying Pilar and Fermina was not their mother — their mother was dead — but their aunt, a sister of Márquez senior. Márquez senior was one of Colombia's leading bankers. Unable to chaperon his children in Europe, he had entrusted them to his sister, who was affectionately called Mama Doloré. She was a Creole aged about forty, who had once been beautiful and who still had in a face now heavy, large, liquid eyes, which were over-intense, pitying in their looks. The three children and their aunt were to stay in France for four years, then spend two years in Madrid, at the end of which they would all return to Bogotá. But there was something which pleased us especially: Mama Doloré and her two nieces were to come and pass every afternoon at Saint Augustine's, until Márquez became accustomed to school life and no longer needed to feel that his family was never far away to help ward off despair.

Thus, we were going to see Fermina Márquez taking walks in the avenues of the grounds every day during the two long afternoon breaks. We had never been afraid of breaking the rules to leave the yard for a smoke in the grounds; and now we had all the more reason . . . We had to return to our prep. The end of this break bore no resemblance to any of the others; life was completely transformed; each of us felt in himself his own high hopes and was astonished to find them so oppressive and so wonderful.

III

We would say to each other: "If someone is to have her, it will be Santos unless that savage Demoisel takes her by force in some corner of the grounds." Iturria himself realized that he had to watch the Negro while courting Fermina at the same time. Besides, ten or so of us contrived to be at the girls' sides.

It was quite simple: after we had appeared in the playground for a few minutes, we would slip out by vaulting the lattice-gate and by inching our way bent double through the foliage of the coppice. Throughout this operation, the younger ones kept a lookout.

In the grounds, we encountered little Márquez walking with his aunt and sisters. We would greet him and bow gracefully to the ladies. Gradually, we came to accompany Mama Doloré and her nieces in a group. But we were always on the alert and ready to hide in the trees at the slightest sign of danger, as some days the monitors were overzealous and came after us.

These strolls were very pleasant. The girls would not talk much but we felt them close to us and Mama Doloré regaled us with wonderful stories of her country; or else she would impart her first impressions of Paris to us and the thousand and one things which surprised her daily. She had rented a large flat in the avenue de Wagram; but she only returned to it to go to bed, because the shops (what a lot of shops!) were too tempting; she and the "little ones" had their meals in restaurants in the centre of town so as not to miss the "bargains"; and then they had to be at Saint Augustine's every day at one o'clock and so . . . "and so the six servants must be having a good time in the avenue Wagram flat!" She was singular, overdressed, wore too much scent, was badly brought-up and charming; she smoked our cigarettes and when she spoke to one of us, she would call him "Queridín" as a lover would do. "Ah for the day when her niece calls me queridín!" Santos used to say.

The parkland opened out in front of us on all sides with its noble avenues – spacious and lofty – between the dense, well-clipped foliage which appeared like walls, terraces of greenery; with its copses where in the play of green, black shadows, the trunks of oaks rose up, swathed in ivy and moss. There were avenues in these grounds of Saint Augustine's worthy of Versailles and Marly. Here and there you could see mighty trees lacerated by cannonball fire from the last war, but which had survived, their great wounds filled in with plasters of tar. And above all, there was the terrace with its vast central staircase and its statue of Saint Augustine all in gilt, dominating the entire valley. This is the valley of the Seine, the domaine of royalty, where the roads and forests seem a continuation of the beautiful parkland and where there is always birdsong. The summer is just beginning: you breathe and the sweetness of France penetrates right to the bottom of your heart.

IV

Near the glasshouse, there was a site laid out for tennis. This was a game for girls, for "yankees", which we looked down on. To appeal to Fermina, Santos and Demoisel invested tennis with a particular prestige. We had racquets and special shoes brought in; it really made a fine picture. Fermina Márquez became very energetic when playing; her strength and agility were wonderful to watch; and she managed to keep an undisturbed dignity and majesty of bearing while engaged at the same time in the most rapid of movements. At that period, wide, open sleeves were being worn; each time the girl raised her arm, her sleeve fell, gradually slipping back beyond her elbow. I am still amazed that she did not sense all our inquiring, hungry looks glued so to speak to her naked arm. One day just after she had returned her racquet to Santos, the game being over, Santos, in front of her, kissed its handle.

"Do you really like racquets as much as that?"

"And the hand which has held them even more."

Santos had taken hold of her wrist and pressed it to his lips. She withdrew her hand sharply and her bracelet, which had become unfastened, fell to the ground. Santos picked it up, saying that he would keep it.

"You wouldn't dare!"

"Oh! I'll do better than that: I'll return it to you at your home in Paris this evening at eleven o'clock."

"You're joking!"

"I promise you. Just tell the caretaker, so that he can let me in and above all don't breathe a whisper of this to the prefect of studies."

"But couldn't this get you expelled?"

Santos shrugged his shoulders and winked at her to indicate that Mama Doloré was approaching, followed by Pilar, Márquez and Léniot, a fifth-form pupil who had earned the trust of the Creole lady by standing up for Márquez against the teasing of his schoolfellows.

Then in an undertone: "Expulsion for this? Ah! I've already tried it – haven't I, blackman?" Demoisel responded with his bizarre laugh: "Ahi, Ahi!"

V

This was the first time that Santos Iturria and Demoisel had publicly referred to their nocturnal escapades. Yet it was an open secret! I have always wondered why they persisted obstinately in saying nothing about it. For two years now it had been going on. Every week on certain days, you could see Iturria and Demoisel coming down from the dormitory at the call to wake up with the washed-out eyes and drawn features of men who have not slept. Looking dog-tired, their ears buzzing, they would appear at prep simply to take a nap behind a barricade of dictionaries. At break, we would not see them either in the yard or in the grounds but when we returned to our classes, we would see them sneak out of the piano practice rooms and conceal themselves in our midst, walking with the heavy step of drowsy people. Santos was pallid, which rather suited him; as for the Negro, he looked like a badly made-up clown, his face smeared with ink and chocolate. In class, they slept once more. Demoisel who was a dunce and who for this reason was seated in the back row, would have a good snooze without putting himself out for anyone, his head resting against the wall, his legs stretched out in front of him. Santos by contrast, who was top of his class, slumbered leaning on his desk, his torso upright. Before falling asleep, he would say to his neighbour: "If I'm asked a question, tap me on the arm." Only in the evenings in the dining hall did they seem to wake up.

And then they would cast each other anxious looks of complicity as though to question whether each was really feeling better. We who guessed the cause of their tiredness, venerated them in silence. This sleepiness which they paraded in front of us a whole day long, this mysterious, conspiratorial behaviour, this air, in short, of men who have "lived it up" all night, aroused our curiosity and made us yearn for pleasures of which we were still ignorant. They were aware of the prestige which these expeditions conferred upon them in our eyes, and I ask myself today whether they did not derive as much satisfaction in showing off their seedy, all-nighter's look to us as in acquiring it while enjoying themselves in the cafés and restaurants of Montmartre. For it was in Montmartre that they used to perform their feats; we had had proof of that: supper bills on the headed paper of well-known restaurants of the Butte had gone round from hand to hand in the philosophy class, bills at the bottom of which the total in francs sometimes came to three figures.

We never knew how they slipped out of the grounds, nor what they had organized so as to return to the dormitory in the middle of the night, barely a few hours before the call to wake up. Had they bought the silence of the night porter, of the night watchmen? Did they have secret dealings with someone in the village? It is more than likely. It was said that the riding master, whose home was outside Saint Augustine's, hired out horses to them. So they rode to the nearest station and in twenty-five minutes or half an hour, the two companions found themselves in Paris. On the return journey, they recovered the horses, left in an inn stable, and did not break a gallop until they reached the school. Fermina Márquez was not wrong: there was enough here to get them expelled and some of the staff sacked at the same time. Anyway, all this only became known to the school authorities much later on, when the culprits and their accomplices had left Saint Augustine's several years before.

Initially, Santos went out by himself at night. He began by frequenting the Quartier Latin, because the train which he used to catch in the suburbs dropped him at place Denfert and he did not yet have the nerve to map out more involved itineraries on the network of orbital trains. But he quickly wearied of the Quartier. He did not feel comfortable in the student brasseries: the milieu was too sophisticated for him; he heard his fellow diners discuss philosophy and literature with astonishment. He felt he was just a schoolboy out of his depth here. Moreover, his immoderate spending, the unconscious flaunting of his money, provoked the spiteful jealousy of the majority and the scorn of one or two of those precisely whom he felt daunted by and whose liking he would have wished to attract. And finally, once he had sampled the costly pleasures of the Butte, he spurned the more modest diversions of the Quartier.

In Montmartre, Santos Iturria could move more freely. Gradually, as he was coming about twice a week, he was numbered in some establishments among the regulars and several of us, after our school careers were over, have met people in the cafés of the boulevard Clichy and place Blanche, who had known M. Iturria and could remember him well.

As soon as Santos had so to speak discovered Montmartre, Demoisel never missed a single spree. Santos had permitted the Negro to accompany him, because, requiring a companion and shrinking from dragging his brother Pablo into these perils, he had found in Demoisel an audacity as great as his own. The two friends became popular in a certain world of revellers, head waiters, gypsies and alluring girls. The Negro, tall, too lanky, with his short nose curiously snubbed at the tip: the irregular but not unattractive nose of a Parisian dressmaker's assistant, but truly remarkable in his African features — an inheritance perhaps from his mother, the 'Pahisian' of Port-au-Prince? — Demoisel, I repeat, nature's oversight, did not have any success with these girls if the truth be known. Moreover he was violent, brutal and malicious, and so strong that nobody dared to contradict him, particularly when he was drunk. At moments such as these, Santos alone was able to restrain him and bring him back to school in time. The other Negroes we had at Saint Augustine's were model pupils; hardworking and highly intelligent, these boys were inoffensive and sparing of words and they had an occasional glimmer of melancholy in their eyes. Demoisel was therefore an exception and a terrible one at that. In certain groups, there were stories told of his deplorable exploits in hushed voices. It seems that, despite Santos, he would enter heaven only knows what dives during these famous nights and pay the girls there to beat them. And these unhappy creatures who doubtless went hungry, acquiesced in this degradation! Today on calm reflection I think this was pure myth, some incident distorted by the imagination of a depraved child. But I well recall the distress this story threw us into, the first time it was related to us. The majority of us were spoilt children and this is what degrades character the most and what hardens the soul, but several amongst us shed tears of indignation and pity on learning of this thing; we used to think about it constantly in spite of ourselves and at night, before falling asleep, it was like a suffocating weight which our hands sought to lift off our chests . . .

Santos, quite on the contrary, was welcome everywhere. No sooner did he enter a restaurant, his head held high, his hat tilted back, than there was always a beautiful woman in some merry group to say: "Well, here's my heartthrob." Santos Iturria was indeed very good-looking. Between eighteen and nineteen years of age, he already had the build, the full-fledged vigour, the confident air of a twenty-five-year-old man. A liveliness normal for his age added, by contrast, a further charm to his appearance. His face was not exactly long, but large, and was always closely shaved which emphasized the characteristics of cleanliness and candour his whole person exuded. His colouring was light, even a little pink. His chestnut hair with its hint of waviness nobly crowned his high

14

brow. But his eyes above all were remarkable: they were blue, but a deep blue which was almost black. They astonished. And all the more so since their unfaltering, manly expression full of gay insolence entirely belied his very long, dark, almost feminine eyelashes.

Santos learnt about life by going to Montmartre to amuse himself in this way. Initially, there had been a certain churlishness in his manners and occasionally he had put himself in the wrong. One evening, as Demoisel and he were running up the stairs of a fashionable restaurant behind a young ladyfriend of theirs, they came across a group of men who were descending this same staircase. The young woman went past, but Santos, wishing to follow, dashed after her and knocked into an elderly man who immediately stood in his way saying: "Sir, I have let the lady go by but it is for you who are young to give way to me now. People have no idea . . . "

The old boy persisted in his reprimand for a few moments and Demoisel was already laughing at the thought of the sharp riposte that Santos was about to make. But Santos meekly listened right to the end. Then he bowed, stepped aside and said unaffectedly: "You are right to rebuke me. I apologize to you Sir."

Somebody on the nearby landing shouted out: "Bravo Sir, you know how to play the game!"

"As for you, I didn't ask for your opinion," retorted Santos and he went past.

Soon, he was able to move with ease in this rather intricate world. He even became a force for the good here: a champion of the disreputable woman and the pet hate of one or two of those mincing fellows seen hanging around certain beautiful girls too much.

These young men are extremely elegant. You enter into conversation with them and they first announce that they are "sons of privileged families" in the process of ruining themselves; they are on the brink of being sought in justice and once they have "squandered" everything, they will blow their brains out. Only, and this is very curious, they will also say: "I am going to tell you an anecdote!" or else, "The atmosphere is heavy this evening"; they have confided that they studied at Janson and yet they have no foreign accent. So you observe them more closely and you note that they appear ill at ease in their tails and speak to the waiters as rudely as is possible. And then when a wealthy man, a *serious client*, seems to find their woman companion pleasing, you see them disappear on some pretext or other, allowing their place to be taken without getting upset. And then you understand (but too late) with whom you have been dealing . . .

Santos Iturria could not stand these fellows of the *demi-monde*. He began by rejecting their overtures with a briskness that did credit to his courage. With great ostentation, he would congratulate the one whose love was sincere on the tact with which he left the way clear for the suitor whose love came at a price in such-and-such a circumstance he recalled. To another, he would speak of love and money with an offensive insistence. His conversation was elegant and highly vivacious; ungossipy but full and adorned with comic expressions, tremendous jokes, delivered with an earnestness which was quite hilarious. And the tone of his voice itself which had something musical would give an added zest to these jests. Soon he took the offensive against these fine fellows he did not like. And with these witless folk, who were quick to anger and to use ugly language, he had a rare time of it. They were his enemies and his butts. He drove them wild. He persecuted them. He made them feel that he was always ready to cuff them as soon as they became crude. And they themselves did not dare to behave boorishly for fear of being shown the door. In these onslaughts of impertinence, Santos invariably had people – both men and women – laughing with him. This was liable to end in real disaster. And one night in the roadway, Santos received a shocking blow on the back of the head. However, Demoisel dealt with the assailant so thoroughly that he did not come back again. Santos recovered from this by spending a few days in the infirmary; as far as everybody was concerned, he had taken a fall in the gymnasium.

Thus, to return Fermina Márquez her bracelet was not really very difficult for Santos. Throughout evening prep and even going upstairs to the dormitory, he played with this bracelet. And the following day when the girl held out her hand to us, the trinket was on her arm. This filled us with pride: Iturria's audacity lent distinction to all of us.

VI

We were now the girl's habitual escort. There were ten or so of us. All those who came near her, those to whom she spoke, with whom she larked about, made up a sort of love's following around her; these were her knights. So the knights of Fermina Márquez were admired by all the pupils and even possibly by the youngest of the monitors. We would no longer bring back the smell of tobacco smoked on the sly from those wonderful walks in the grounds, but rather the fragrance of the young South American girls. Was it geranium or mignonette? It was an indefinable scent, a scent which conjured up blue, mauve, white and pink dresses; large, floppy straw hats; dark hair in ringlets or curled like shells; black eyes so huge that the whole sky must be mirrored in them.

Pilar was only a child; her fingers were always stained with ink, her elbows chafed – those blatant, fatuous signs of little girls aged between eleven and thirteen. But Fermina really was a grown-up girl. It is for this reason that her appearance had something which so affected us. A girl! On seeing her, we would want to clap our hands and dance around her. So what is it that sets her apart from a young woman to such an extent? I watch a young woman, a young mother surrounded by her children, and she watches me in turn and recognizes me: it is my hand which drew her and only released her once I had received her kiss. She watches me and has all these images stored within her: I am a man, similar to the father of her children. Whereas for the girl, I am an unfamiliar person, a strange country, an enigma. A poor, unfamiliar person, all clumsiness and stammers in her presence; a pitiful mystery who loses his entire composure at a peal of her laughter.

And yet we are not so unfamiliar to each other: when life leaves me quite alone with myself, I discover aspirations and feelings of a woman within me; and I am sure that those women who know how to explore themselves, can perceive the lucid and well-ordered mind of man beyond their own bountiful woman's heart. But since we will never be able to understand ourselves clearly, will we ever come to know that part of the opposite sex which we all contain, both men and women? At twenty, it was our mistake to believe that we had fathomed life and womankind. Neither the one nor the other will ever be fathomed; only objects of astonishment and an uninterrupted succession of miracles prevail everywhere. Santos thought he had got to know about women in the cafés of Montmartre; and we too who had only gone – and then infrequently – to tea parties and soirées at the houses of our guardians in Paris, we too would say to ourselves: "That's a woman all over."

VII

However, the scandal of our absence at break; our unsanctioned walks and our games of tennis in the grounds finally disturbed the school authorities. And one day, each of Fermina Márquez' knights heard that he had been forbidden entrance to the grounds on pain of the most severe disciplinary action. Léniot, a fifth-form pupil, was alone given special permission to accompany these ladies. Mama Doloré had asked this favour because Léniot had become the protector of little Márquez and was steering him through the early pitfalls of school life.

VIII

Joanny Léniot, at fifteen and a half, was quite simply a schoolboy good at composition. His physiognomy was not pleasant; he was taciturn and never looked people straight in the face. He lived, moreover, in relative isolation. He was even suspected of using break to go over his lessons in his head, while all the time pretending to sleep stretched out on a bench. He had a somewhat drab nature about which nobody would have been able to say anything precise. He was there, sitting in his place or standing in his row; that was all. But on prizegiving day when his class was read out, none but his name would be heard, he alone could be seen on the rostrum; and since in the end he was a credit to the school, all the pupils applauded him with such vigour they would hurt their hands. Yet nobody liked him.

He had come to Saint Augustine's when he was nine, barely able to read. At first, he had felt so lonely — surrounded by these schoolfellows who spoke a language unfamiliar to him — so like a captive, so abandoned that he had begun to work frantically to stop being affected by the wretchedness of his existence. He started to study as a man might start to drink: to forget. He was one of those characters whom a boarding school can stamp with an ineradicable flaw; he knew it and did his best to struggle against its influence.

His progress astounded everybody. At the end of one year,

he was moved from the juniors' penultimate class into the senior school's first form, and in this new class he came top in the first composition of the year. From that moment on he dug his heels in, determined never to lose first place. He had been excluded from outdoor games; his clumsiness guaranteed the defeat of his side; the team captains themselves asked that he be excused from participating in the games. Of this he was glad. Henceforth, nothing interested him except this first place, his *idée fixe*. And it was an unstinting daily effort, for even the ordinary prepared work was given an order of merit after it had been corrected. The actual subject matter of his studies hardly mattered to him: science, literature, grammar, geography, they were simply opportunities for satisfying his obsession with scholastic distinction. He could have been taught anything at all since this ambition had been kindled in him. This goal blinded him; he had reached the point of no longer experiencing life's daily movement around him, of no longer seeing its monotony, its dullness and banality: the prep monitor who yawns over the authors he is studying for his degree, the idlers who are rushing slapdash through their proses and the dunces who are catching flies or gazing wistfully out of the windows, where a mother-of-pearl sky deepens to the blue of night. The melancholy of those evenings at Saint Augustine's no longer even made any impression on him — those forlorn village evenings of the outer suburbs, when you can hear until sleep overcomes you the distant moaning of trains which seem to flee towards Paris terror-stricken . . . Joanny Léniot's every effort was strained to what he used to call, in his heart of hearts, success.

And so this is what would happen: the boys would return to their classes; the master would be seated at his desk; in front of him, a pile of corrected scripts. Once silence had fallen, he would say: "I have given 18 out of 20 to Mr Léniot's unseen: it is without any real errors; I will read it out to you."

Or else, it would be the results of the last composition. They were only given in each form every week on Saturday evening in the presence of the prefect of studies and a chief monitor. They would begin with the highest forms: the upper and lower sixths . . . For a quarter of an hour, twenty minutes, Joanny Léniot, seated at his desk, listened to the different stages of the ceremony. The sounds of footsteps and voices, the pupils' din as they all stood up at the same time on the entrance of the authorities – he heard all this and his doubts and anxieties drove him out of his mind. And these noises would be repeated from one class to the next. Now these gentlemen were entering the formroom next door. Finally it would be the turn of Léniot's class. In frock coats and top hats, the authorities made their entrance; the pupils and master stood up.

"Sit down, gentlemen," said the prefect of studies who assumed a solemn expression. And then the master would read out the results of the last composition. What a moment!

"First: Léniot (Joanny)."

He hurriedly got to his feet; the prefect of studies smiled at him; then he sat down again shakily. It caused an upheaval, a shock to his mind, an unhinging of his nervous system. Until the end of the class, he continued to tremble inside from this, to retain a sort of feverishness. At the doorway, he would hear: "Did you have an order called in your form? Who came top?" "Léniot again of course!"

He allowed no trace of his joy to surface. Besides, he knew how little all that mattered to the vast majority of the pupils. And he did wish to be modest as well. But this joy was so great that he wanted to cry out, that he walked with stooping gait, wholly bent beneath the weight of his pride. Just as in the pictures of adventure stories a pirate can be seen carrying a beautiful white girl captive, so it seemed to him as though he were walking dazzled, holding his glory in his arms right against his heart. It was a fresh victory: for a further eight days, he would be seated in the form's place of honour. It was a bit like after Communion: he felt purified; he had more respect for himself.

The prefect of studies and all the masters used to congratulate him: high hopes were founded on him. He was so intelligent, he absorbed everything so quickly. This was the widely held opinion, for Joanny Léniot had the pride to conceal his dogged exertions. If he permitted himself a slack half an hour in prep, he would spend it demonstrating to everyone how idle he was, by getting up twenty times from his place, by having himself constantly admonished by the monitor. He would affect to copy out his prepared work at the last minute. He even managed to sleep during lessons. All this was deceptive and his mental swiftness aroused wonderment. In fact, his emotions were always more lively and distinct than his thoughts; they obscured his intelligence which was dominated by them, and all in all, despite his reputation for being intellectually able, Léniot was remarkable only for his boundless ambition, which truly was above that of his peers.

His parents (who lived in Lyons) used to write him letters of encouragement, full of praise for each of his successes. Léniot senior would tell himself that his son understood the sacrifices being made for him, and that as a sensible boy he would take advantage of the education which was being placed within his reach. And his mother would reflect: "It's to please me that he works so much!" Joanny discerned these thoughts behind their congratulations. No, his parents would never understand . . . and he tore up their letters with smiles of pity. Nobody would ever understand that what he wanted and what he worked so hard for was solely this upheaval of the mind, this spasm occurring in response to the call of glory: "First: Léniot (Joanny)". These insignificant little feats of a schoolboy with a good record became the triumphs of a Roman emperor in his adolescent imagination.

Yet the adult world does not guess — life has so deafened, so blunted it — that these laurels might well never fade on the brow of this gifted pupil. At Saint Augustine's, wreaths were not awarded at prizegiving; but engraved on their covers, the books bore escutcheons in gold, set with the school's initials:

24

S.A. which, according to the old pun handed down from generation to generation since the school's earliest days, also meant: Sleazy Alehouse. The escutcheon was about as wide as a hundred-franc piece. For a long time, Joanny had gazed reverentially at this golden disc. It was like the permanent reflection of the memorable "first ray of glory" of which several fine authors speak; and although this deference was already nothing more than a childhood memory for him, at the mere sight of his prize books from the preceding years, his boyhood stood revealed with all its bitter taste, sadness and earnestness. Yet, throughout his life he would have prizes; throughout his life he would feel the warmth of this golden disk resting on him. His whole life would breathe that studious gravity, that quiet, unremitting tenacity to excel in everything. For him, his whole life would have that precious bitterness, the bay leaf's self-same savour. And outside, far from prep rooms and dark corridors, there might be the vast open air and the whole summer with its full-scented breezes which make you dizzy; or again, there might be the autumn and the first warm mists which settle like a hand on your heart; there might be Paris and all its nights full of sins – such wonderful, such terrible sins, you would not dare imagine them; there might be all the women of the earth, who are so beautiful that you would want to find them names to express their beauty; and there might be Fermina Márquez' eyes, in which the tropical sun dazzles; – Joanny Léniot turned his face to the wall and thinking of the prepared work he had to do, experienced in his innermost self a joy which was greater than all these joys.

No, he would not be disturbed for anything in the world. His would be a centralization of the self, a refusal to overdiversify, to grant a moment's sympathy to anything whatsoever. He could plainly see the limitations of his mind. He had read and reread a short *Life of Benjamin Franklin*, which had ended with these words: "he wrung the most he could out of himself". Léniot would reflect: "Franklin must have despised himself as I myself do; but he found the way to be great in the eyes of men . . . that is the path to follow and without faltering". He was sparing of himself. When Fermina Márquez appeared at the school bringing with her a fresh spirit, he admitted that he had allowed himself to be distracted for an instant. The most wonderful eyes in the world were not supposed to divert him from his commendable goal. Had Caesar so much as on a single occasion looked fondly at the daughters or wives of the Gaulish chieftains? When from the ramparts' top, they entreated him by exposing their breasts; or again, when on the evening of a battle they were brought in herds to the proconsul's camp, had he ever experienced the slightest thrill of pity, a moment of desire for the prettiest and most unfortunate of them? Nevertheless, they were absolutely his to command; and they sensed their master perfectly in this diminutive, bald, well-shaven man! How often Joanny had imagined scenes of this sort . . .

Well then, he himself just like Caesar was destined to be admired by men and loved by women. It was unworthy of him to admire and love in return. Or rather, perhaps he could love but only a captive woman, that is to say one humbled and imploring who grovelled at your feet and fearfully kissed your hands. Yes, but could such a woman be found anywhere other than in novels whose actions took place in the colonies?

Not having a sister, seeing little of girls, Léniot instinctively recoiled from those pert creatures who, with their mockery, so severely test the timid and solemn pride of very young men. It is pretty hard for a boy who compares himself exclusively with the likes of Franklin and Julius Caesar to hear himself ridiculed for a blunder committed while serving tea, or for the over-vivid green of a new tie. Bursting with resentment, he did not forget the memory of occasions when he had been a laughingstock and when inane, older girls had made fun of him, "silly little geese, provincial peasants with their rustic tones". But the evocation of their accent was not enough to avenge Léniot for the wounds they had inflicted on his self-esteem. No – and as he drew closer to his sixteenth year, he became more convinced of this — what would truly give him his revenge, what would conclusively fix his position and his attitude towards women was a *seduction*. By this expedient, from the child he was at the outset, he would become a man; then unquestionably he would at last be able to approach those as yet uninitiated little fools without blushing. By this expedient as well, he would experience a new kind of triumph: he would know what a man feels to see a girl sacrifice her scruples, sense of decency and all her years of innocence for him. "And a woman who gives herself, isn't she failing her entire sex?" Yes, just seduce one of them! How your conqueror's heart beats feverishly at this thought!

So Léniot mused as he smoked his after-lunch cigarette in the grounds. At this precise moment, Mama Doloré and the young Colombian girls appeared round an avenue. Léniot hastened to join them and, while greeting them, looked Fermina implacably in the face as one would an enemy. The thought had just occurred to him: "Why shouldn't it be you?"

Suddenly the temerity of this idea struck him; it seemed to him as though all his blood were sweeping back in flight towards his heart. This girl was so beautiful, so arrestingly graceful and majestic in her youthfulness that he would never dare even allow her to see the confusion into which her presence threw him. And then, just as abruptly, his will reasserted itself and drove the overheated, altogether electrified blood back into his veins. Oh yes! He dared; he would show them! He began to walk at her side. He could envisage everything he proposed to accomplish. With care, he measured the distance separating him from the first kiss. And here once again his courage failed him. Yet where was the urgency? But now he came up against an obstacle which his timidity — quivering and recalcitrant — refused to clear. It was not that he was afraid of setting himself up as Santos Iturria's rival. On the contrary; even were it to end with a fight in which he, Léniot, would certainly be beaten, he would keep the very considerable prestige of having defied the school hero all on his own . . . "and over a woman as well". Nor was it that he thought he might be treated as a child and disregarded because of his age; besides, Fermina Márquez was barely a year older than him. So whence did this obstacle stem if not from his own timidity? And yet he did not lack pluck. The essential point was to make a start; and this was bound to be simple; even amongst the classical writers, their lovers appeared to feel no embarrassment in declaring their love. Moreover, Santos and Ortega and other pupils in the upper forms would frequently visit the linen room to steal kisses off the young linen maids one after another. To be sure, this only involved linen maids. But one morning, in the dining hall, Pablo boasted that he had slipped love letters into the hands of their young female guests at the time of last Saint Charlemagne's day, yes love letters, and under the noses of their parents. And one of them had even replied — what more could a gallant man say?

She had replied.

"So why should I waver?" said Léniot to himself.

IX

He waited for evening prep, for the end of his working day to go back over it all, to organize his ideas and test the constancy of his resolve. It was precisely on that evening that the supervision of prep had been entrusted for the first time to a young tutor, Mr Lebrun, who had entered the school's service a week previously. It is difficult to imagine the anxiety and irritation of a young tutor who is just starting out; it is impossible to conceive of the sort of dizziness overcoming him when he sees himself quite alone with his back to the wall on a rostrum, facing and slightly looking down at forty youngsters aged between fifteen and seventeen. Mr Lebrun was especially agitated. In the lower classes, he had been dreadfully "baited" and it was specifically for this reason that he had asked to supervise a more responsible prep group − this one, which comprised the pupils of the fifth and a part of the sixth forms. Léniot thought that this new monitor would not dare to disrupt his idleness; so comfortably propped up at his desk, he concentrated his mind on the matter which had been occupying him for several hours.

First of all, there was this timidity which he had to subdue. But it was no longer just timidity, it was terror! And it was a terror which blinded him, which would cause him to squander the most heaven-sent opportunities for speech or action. He regretted not being properly in love; then perhaps this conquest would be easy for him. But confronted by the difficulty of the undertaking, any feelings of tenderness or affection evaporated and the thought of Fermina Márquez was irksome to him, even became painful and humiliated him. Just as a horse is led back to the object which frightens it, so Joanny patiently coaxed his will to face this image of Fermina Márquez he had in his mind and had ended up by finding intolerable.

"Why aren't you working then?"

"Me Sir?" said Léniot, brought back to the present.

"Yes you! Your name if you please?" asked Mr Lebrun, striving to steady his voice.

"Léniot."

"Well then Mr Léniot, will you please work?"

Mr Lebrun was being over-zealous. With the younger prep groups, he had expected that he would be provoked; here he supposed he would make himself respected by taking the offensive. He was incessantly calling somebody to order; and without knowing whether he was dealing with a good or a lazy pupil, he reprimanded schoolboys whom it was unusual to hear being treated like dunces. And he thought he saw in Léniot, completely idle that evening, the prep group's most trying character.

Joanny shrugged his shoulders and pursued his own thoughts . . . What then were the causes of this timidity? The principal one was undoubtedly this notion – which his mother and all the women in his family had instilled in him – namely that a fundamental, intrinsic disparity forever separates honest women from the rest. They were two different sexes so to speak. You respected the one; as for the other, "you paid", no more need be said. This view was undisputed and universally held by his mother and the middle-class women of her circle. But in his case, it had naturally been undermined by the education he was receiving at school. Indeed, this wholly bourgeois distinction is unknown to great writers: they exalt abandoned and virtuous women indiscriminately. They even prefer to choose women as their heroines whose passions and excesses have made them famous: Medea, Dido, Phaedra. Occasionally, Joanny would amuse himself by imagining grotesque parallels between these celebrated lovers and the ladies who came to tea at his mother's. The characteristics of the honest woman were ugliness, stupidity, bitchiness. By contrast, the other, the despised one, was beautiful, intelligent and giving. Without any doubt whatsoever, it was primordial man in his masculinity who had established this distinction and who in his own interest had imposed it on his companion. Thus, under man's domination, the fair sex was just like a well-supervised herd, so well-trained indeed, that it had succeeded in doing its own policing and in instinctively driving all the unruly types, all the black sheep out of its ranks. Joanny did not ask himself whether this law was just or unjust, nor whether it was not in women's interests to conform to it; however, he observed that women heeded this law, blindly duped by their eternal master, the grasping lord of the patriarchal era, the Roman husband *cum manu*. All in all, there was no very great difference: "some are called subservient outside marriage and others like my mother and her friends are subservient within marriage; that is all." — Joanny was pleased with this choice of words; at fifteen, he was proud of having ideas of this sort; he thought them original and daring. At the same time, the old scruples of the pious child in him reproached him for the irreverence towards his mother which his thoughts revealed. Certainly, Léniot's notion of the honest woman had been gravely impaired. But it survived as a central distinction between two modes of education. In the final analysis, all differences could be reduced to that. There were the properly brought-up women and there were the rest. And the basis of the attraction of girls in his eyes was precisely that they formed a third group. They still had to choose between vice and virtue and they derived their appeal from both. Fermina Márquez was a girl; and it was just that which disconcerted Joanny in particular: he thought he would have

31

ventured everything with a young woman. Well then, yet another reason to attempt the seduction of the little South American . . .

Anyway, it would most certainly be better for him not to be in love at all. He was not for anything in the world to lapse into sentimental foolishness: repeating mawkish passages from novels; endeavouring to compose a sonnet and discovering that the sonnet of Arvers has been transcribed almost word for word; daydreaming; and all that has been achieved is to waste time. No, Joanny had to apply his full store of methodical patience, all the studious obstinacy of the model pupil to this bid at seduction. He had to be dispassionately calculating, to keep an eye on events, to watch out for opportunities . . .

Meanwhile, prep was becoming rowdy. Mr Lebrun, in a panic, was now reprimanding continuously. Joanny heard his neighbour mutter: "This idiot isn't even letting us get on quietly with our work."

"You persist in doing nothing, Mr Léniot?" asked Mr Lebrun aggressively.

"I am meditating, Sir," answered Joanny.

The entire prep group began to laugh openly. Hearing the monitor being held up to ridicule by the foremost pupil acted as the spur. A bait was organized.

"Have you quite finished talking to your neighbour, Mr Zuniga?" shouted the monitor.

"Come now Mr Montemayor!"

"What? I'm being very well behaved, Sir."

"Hey you, yes you there. Your name please."

"Juan Bernardo de Claraval Marti de la Cruz y del Milagro de la Concha."

The laughter turned into howls of merrriment.

Joanny's excitement rose in this hubbub. The desire for a scrap came to him, as did an audacity which made his timidity towards Fermina Márquez seem absurd. He devised the simplest of seduction plans. First of all, he contemplated writing a fine letter imbued with respect and affection like the one with which *La Nouvelle Héloïse* begins. Then he thought that a short note would be better. Finally, he decided not to write at all but to present himself straightforwardly as a friend, and as a friend to the whole Márquez family. Initially, it was of the first importance to gain the trust of Mama Doloré. And for that, he had to become her nephew's friend and protector.

As it happened, little Márquez, a spoilt child, wholly lacked tact in his relations with his schoolfellows. He regarded Saint Augustine's as a hotel, a far less luxurious one than the English and French hotels in which he had lived since leaving Bogotá it is true, but for all that he regarded it as a hotel where payment procured service. And Mama Doloré gave him too much pocket money. Instead of responding to those teasing him with his fists, he would hand out sweetmeats to them, hoping by this means to be left alone. Unfortunately, the outcome of this ploy was not the one he had been counting on. His tormentors returned to tease him more than ever. So he would call them tramps and beggars and boast about his father's wealth: "We came as far as Southampton in our very own ship," he used to shout with pride. Finally, one day he was dragged beneath the pump in the yard and drenched. Those who had soaked Márquez were placed in isolation. No snub was spared him. He spent the greater part of his nights choking back his sobs, his head buried under his bolster. He had already lost a lot of weight. In a few days, Léniot could put all that to rights. He would do so. That was the real way of insinuating himself into this family. Afterwards, he would see . . . There were still two and a half months before the summer holidays.

Joanny stood up, in euphoria. He felt a sort of debonair impatience which he had experienced as yet only once; on the day before his departure for Italy last Easter break. He was unable to remain in his place; he would have liked to be able to sing.

Without asking for Mr Lebrun's permission, he went and took Schrader's large atlas from the prep room's bookcase and looked up the map of Colombia in it.

"Mr Léniot, for having moved without permission you will be given nought for conduct."

Joanny smiled disdainfully. He studied the geographical outline of the Colombian republic with care, as if he had planned a trip in this country. The principal port on the Caribbean Sea was called Cartagena; it was from here that she must have left. The prep group had fallen silent for a moment, astonished to hear a black mark being given to the best pupil for the first time. The expression on Léniot's face was observed with curiosity. But Mr Lebrun pursued his advantage. He was handing out a stream of "noughts for conduct". And the rowdiness of the bait intensified. At the end of the room where he was seated, Pablo Iturria raised the lid of his desk then let it come down again with a resounding crash and, turning to the monitor, bellowed: "Calla, hombre, calla!"

Joanny, who had not stopped smiling, returned to his seat. He was full of self-confidence. Above all, he felt safe, whatever happened. "Even supposing the worst, my father is the last person to reproach me for having seduced the daughter of a millionnaire!" he said to himself. He saw his whole life stretching out in front of him as an inexhaustible stock of success and happiness.

"Mr Léniot, you do appreciate that a report will be sent to the prefect of studies along with your nought for conduct."

The nervous exhilaration which had until then borne Joanny up, plummeted all of a sudden: this black mark and report meant that he would be excluded from the roll of honour — they meant a detention, ultimately the loss of the prize for excellence and the ruin of his school career! No, this was out of the question! He pulled himself together, he had to act.

He belonged to a matchless generation which was to leave the memory of unsurpassable audacity and virility to those who were now in the lower classes. What he was going to do would put his name in the same rank as those of the two Iturrias, of Ortega, of those of the finest representatives of this much-vaunted generation. Or conversely, if he were not successful, he would be universally regarded as deceitful and placed in isolation – no, he would quite simply be thrown out of the school. He did not stop to think for a single moment that he might wreck Mr Lebrun's career, perhaps cause him to be dismissed by the administration. He had these words of command circulated: "Continue the bait; I am going to get the prefect of studies."

Then he left the room without condescending to reply to the remark sarcastically flung at him by the monitor whose patience was exhausted: "Don't bother to wait to be told to leave the room, will you? Just go as you please; it's something you have got used to."

Léniot crossed the yard, the grounds and rang the doorbell of the chalet where the prefect of studies lived with his family. Admitted to the presence of the school's most senior official, he related what was going on in the prep room of the new monitor. Normally, they were a trustworthy group; there had never been a cause for complaint. Mr Lebrun was alone responsible for the disturbance.

With gravity, the prefect of studies listened to Joanny's plea. This step was extraordinary. The pupil who had taken it was one of the best in the school. The prefect of studies hesitated to make a final judgement. He wanted to see for himself and followed Léniot. Thus, as he had promised, Léniot brought the prefect of studies back with him. His triumph was more than half complete. As they entered, the whole prep group was standing up jeering at the tutor.

A silence fell abruptly. Under the eyes of his companions and Mr Lebrun, Léniot renewed his diatribe against the monitor. His tone of voice was restrained but quite resolute and the prefect of studies did not interrupt him. From time to time, Mr Lebrun made objections, but clumsily:

"The younger Iturria insulted me in Spanish!"

"You're lying!" retorted Pablo.

"You have just called us louts!" shouted a pupil. Léniot

drew to a conclusion:

"Mr Lebrun, by his excessive use of reprimands and black marks, has been the sole cause of this disturbance. We leave you Sir, the prefect of studies, with the responsibility for making him understand this."

The prefect of studies did not want to appear as embarrassed as he really was. He clearly saw that tempers had risen.

"Gentleman," he said, "I have come . . . "

He was cut short by applause. This was discreet and brief, conveying respect, gratitude and trust.

For all the world, the prefect of studies would not have wished to find himself at odds with his South American boarders whom he called − but strictly in private − "my toreadors". From the moment he started to speak, he was expected to be conciliatory and unreservedly lenient.

"Pupils of the fifth and sixth forms, you ought to be ashamed of yourselves for having behaved like primary school children" . . . Iturria minor ought to realize that it is the height of rudeness to talk to somebody in a language which that person cannot understand at all . . . Mr Lebrun showed justifiable severity . . . Moreover, Mr Léniot rightly took advantage of his authority as a model pupil to inform him of what was happening in this prep room. He himself was personally sure that discipline would be respected here in the future. Mr Lebrun was a man of distinction; hard-working and with a rare intellect. He, the prefect of studies, hoped to see a certain affinity develop between master and pupils. He was convinced that this affinity could develop quickly.

Besides, the sixth-form boys were only two months away from their exams; they therefore had to work harder than ever . . . The black marks and punishments noted down by Mr Lebrun would be upheld; but Mr Lebrun would be free to lift them at the end of the week if his pupils' conduct satisfied him . . . The incident was closed.

The prefect of studies shook Mr Lebrun by the hand, led him into the passage for a few seconds and moved off.

Mr Lebrun was astonished to see his charges calm down. The prefect of studies' soothing words had brought about this radical transformation. For all this, he remained no less vanquished in his struggle with the prep group. According to all the school rules, the entire lot ought to be kept in: the instigators placed in detention rooms and Léniot made to await the summons of the disciplinary committee. The punishments and black marks would be quashed, that was quite certain. One or two unrepentant types might regret that the bait had come to an end so soon. But the majority of the pupils were pleased with Léniot's intervention.

Dust had yet to settle in the room — the exhilarating, eye-stinging dust which follows a battle. Joanny, standing in his place, briefly summed up the incident, recalled the propitiatory words of the prefect of studies, then held out his hand to Mr Lebrun who was almost apologetic. The marks would be excellent this evening! In his turn, Pablo went up to the rostrum and in a few minutes of hushed discussion with Mr Lebrun, patched up their disagreement.

Joanny Léniot could read his victory in everybody's eyes. The prefect of studies really did seem to present his extraordinary action as the work of a sneak but no one was taken in by this. It was a great success: the South Americans wholeheartedly approved of the deed. But the main point was that Joanny would not have the black mark which would have caused his name to be removed from the roll of honour. Like a gambler who has hazarded the last of his purse and has finally won, he remained slightly dazed, too enraptured for his joy to burst out immediately.

Again after such a feat, everything appeared so straightforward to him. Were she there, he would already have declared himself. But once again, there was no hurry. A seduction was an undertaking of method, patience and profound calculation. "*That* and the prize for excellence," what a wonderful end to the school year! . . .

A drum roll summoned all the pupils to the refectory; after

a quickly taken supper they returned to their prep rooms for a quarter of an hour and, once prayers had been said, the drum boomed again for bedtime. The din of the pupils going up to the dormitories filled the corridors and stairways. Joanny was on the look-out for the second-form boys, for the lower classes filed past the top forms who would stand waiting outside their prep rooms and go up last of all. With the noise of their footfall and the sounds of their voices, the younger ones walked jauntily past, in close order, large eyes gleaming here and there from out of the shadows. With jokes and smiles exchanged amongst themselves and calls of goodnight by the juniors to the senior boys, this was the one moment of the day when we were truly gentle and good. As the second formers were going by, Léniot slipped in amongst them and followed little Márquez who was walking at the front. There was a sudden jostling on the staircase; somebody overtook Márquez, pushed him brutally out of the way and made him fall. So Léniot was able to step up to him; he helped him to his feet again and proffered him his beret, which had rolled on to the staircase. Márquez took the beret, stammered out his thanks and continued on his way up.

"*Y el panuelo tambien,*" said Léniot holding out his handkerchief which he had just picked up.

Little Márquez looked at Léniot for the first time. And his glance was full of astonishment. Sorrowfully, he attempted to smile. Then Joanny hesitated no longer; he took him by the hand, leant towards him and embraced him. Márquez struggled, wanting to break free; his pride mutinied. But he had met with so much harshness, so much actual cruelty since entering the school, that this mark of affection — and coming as it did from a senior — broke down all his courage, all his unflinching resignation to suffering. He restrained himself no more, laid his head against the breast of this friend and vented in sobs the full store of his anguish.

Meanwhile, the two of them, entwined together and merged in with the crowd of pupils, had not stopped their upward progress. Léniot tried to find words appropriate to the circumstances; but he was unable. A triumphal joy over-whelmed him. He savoured the calmness he was feeling, the perfection with which he was playing this role of the comforter. He wondered what would happen if, holding the child as he was to his heart, he were to burst out laughing all of a sudden. This was no doubt what it was like to "enjoy peaceful tranquillity in the act of crime". Yes, this had been neatly done! Words would spoil everything. He felt a superiority over everything around him and despised this despair he was alleviating. "Yet what if his sister were to see us?" he mused. He was delighted by his own heartlessness! At the door of the second form's dormitory, Léniot embraced Márquez again, gave the burning little hand a tight squeeze and murmured quite simply: "See you tomorrow Paquito." Nobody had been watching them.

Every evening before falling asleep, he was in the habit of recalling his speech and actions of the past day and to pass judgement on them. He examined them coldy and did not seek to find excuses for them. Well, then, that evening, he realized that he really had fewer grounds for self-congratulation than he had at first thought. His intervention in the disturbance at the prep room was not the heroic action he had supposed when concocting it. There was something hypocritical about it, though he would not have been able to say precisely in what particular respect it was so. Unquestion-ably the Iturrias, with their unswerving notion of school honour, would not have behaved in quite this way. In short, he had exposed all his school fellows to serious punishment, in order to have a black mark which he had deserved, struck out in his own interest. Fortunately, it had all passed off without mishap. But he had certainly revealed an unattractive side of his character to the prefect of studies, for the latter's speech, if his choice of phrase were to be considered more closely, was a great deal more subtle than it first appeared. Without a doubt, the prefect of studies had in an instant discerned the shabby effrontery deep down in the heart of "this model pupil".

"Oh damn! He has seen through me for the time being."

But what did it matter to Joanny that he had merited this man's contempt, if this contempt were not translated into an opposition to his scholastic success? He only regretted that he had not pushed his hypocrisy to the point where it escaped detection. He felt that if he had to behave vilely to protect his rights to the prize for excellence, he would have done so without compunction. Discontented to find that his was not a perfectly honest character, he rushed headlong to the opposite extreme and was not displeased to see himself as the villain of a melodrama.

But the thought of Fermina Márquez intruded to alter the course of this self-examination. The thought of Ferminita is the most wonderful you can have. And then there is the desire to be Ferminita's beloved. Yet just to see her, or rather to know or to have known her, suffices to lend a poetic glow to an entire existence. Liners cross the Atlantic. Later when we have grown to manhood, we will go to South America. We will see all the women there with eyes which have beheld Fermina Márquez. There is a proverb which says that the women of Lima are the most tender of all; there are also the popular lovesongs of the Argentine Republic, like *Vidalita* for example, which are so despairing of love! . . . At this moment, as Joanny is coldly calculating his chances, merely the idea that you exist, Fermina, is enough to console every little boy who has gone to bed with a heavy heart because he has been punished for the first time or because a fellow pupil, stronger than he is, is tyrannizing over him . . . And it is certain as well that all the words of Argentinian ballads and *habaneras* have been written for you.

On the next day during the first break, as little Márquez came up to him, Léniot experienced all the feelings a young man can, when a boy, his friend, bestows upon him all the natural affection of his heart. But this was a role he was playing after all and he was not going to allow himself to be

40

touched by this. A few blows dispensed at the right moment deterred Márquez' persecutors. Two weeks later, following the events narrated above, he found himself the possessor of all the affection and trust which Mama Doloré was able to give to a stranger; he became the family's only companion during its walks in the grounds of Saint Augustine's and almost straight away the sole confidant of Fermina Márquez.

X

Mama Doloré soon left the young people alone together; she was tired of them. She would walk slowly between Pilar and her nephew, smoking and hardly talking at all. She had said to Joanny and Fermina: "You will speak French together, won't you? *La Chica* absolutely must learn to speak faultlessly."

Joanny gladly assented to this wish. Speaking his own language, he had two advantages over his partner in conversation: he could nuance his remarks to an infinite degree and he could pull her up if she made mistakes. And, confined to a more limited vocabulary, she would express her thoughts more ingenuously.

The first day alone had the magic of an adventure and it was so feverish and gay, above all so gay, that in the evening Joanny was overpowered by that deep and ill-defined sadness which comes at the end of a holiday or a day in the country, when for a whole afternoon there has been too much joking and laughter. He had come out of himself for a few dazzling hours and now he was once again crossing the threshold of his soul like a man returning from the theatre to his dark, deserted home at night. The place he had come from was so brilliant that he could no longer make anything out in his everyday life. He had a moment's hesitation; he could not remember any more what only a short while before was binding him so intensely to his life; his concerns were of no further interest to him.

He wanted to go back to the Greek unseen he had started; it was a poem of Tyrtaeus and so beautiful that the alexandrines materialized in French, without prompting, to match the Greek verse. Greek unseens, indeed exercises in general, have their own particular features; the difficulty lies not so much in the text itself as in the way it is presented and the style in which it is to be translated. Joanny took a hard look at his Greek unseen and no longer found it intelligible. How could he have been fascinated by this gibberish? These very alterations had been lovingly done. And now it was a worthless piece of scrap paper. The pointlessness of these exercises suddenly struck Joanny: rough drafts, corrected copies! Without cease, they vanished into nothingness. So many hours spent doing them and so much care lavished! Was it possible that there was nothing to show for it all? For the first time, Joanny perceived the futility of his labour. He understood the superior wisdom of the idler. His ambition seemed to him so far away that evening! He resumed the translation of Tyrtaeus but without enthusiasm, like a chore to accustom himself to his existence once again. He had no precise reason for feeling sombre; it was as if he had used up all his reserves of joy and found sadness at the bottom.

No, he had no reason for feeling sombre; on the contrary. However, he had been disappointed. Fermina Márquez was not the person he had imagined her to be; girls, as a rule, were not as he had imagined them. He had gone out to meet Fermina Márquez, as one would the enemy, feeling thoroughly terrified as well as overwhelmingly brave. And the enemy had advanced towards him with her hand out; instead of an armed warrior, he had found a good friend, and better still, a good friend who was female. He had been grateful to her for sparing him this combat for which he had gone to such lengths to prepare himself. But the change of attitude which by the same token was imposed upon him was disconcerting at first. He saw all his plans crumble: would he therefore have to be satisfied with a simple friendship? Everything seemed to be called into question.

But the girl had spoken and he had been obliged to answer her. And Joanny, soothed, his nerves unwound, had a foretaste of the great pleasure those conversations give, so childlike and so intense, those serious and innocent secrets which girls and boys of fifteen exchange – and afterwards, nevermore.

The remarkable thing was that she had not made fun of him. Then she had astonished him by saying: "You Frenchmen are so difficult to understand; it takes so little for you to go from high spirits to melancholy. It is impossible ever to guess the motives for your actions. I think you must be the most peculiar of all foreigners."

Joanny felt great pride in exciting the girl's curiosity. "She's going to observe me," he thought. He would have wished to behave in an uncommon fashion on purpose; but was too afraid of being ridiculous.

They had talked, as they strolled in step at each other's sides on the terrace. Their ideas met and they might have described their respective imaginations as two birds flying together along the avenues of the grounds right to the furthest recesses of the foliage. And Joanny savoured this caressing of his mind which he had not envisaged. Fermina Márquez was something more than just a girl who had to be seduced: she had an existence of her own which could not be disregarded.

She had said some other extraordinary things:

"Don't your studies lead you away from humility?"

This ingenuousness was worthy of a boy. Another thing: she had compared the school buildings to a great liner:

" . . . A great liner like the ones which provide the service between Europe and America. Even the life you lead here makes one think of it; you eat at set times and say prayers together."

"No," Joanny had replied, "the resemblance lies in the fact that we cannot leave school any more than the passengers can the liner, once it's moving. I too had this idea when I was first here and shut in. If you're in the prep rooms, dormitories, anywhere ultimately where you can't see the grounds or the road running past the entrance gate, you can easily imagine that you are in an enormous ship out on the open sea."

"And the noise of the generator supplying the electricity is the noise of the engines, don't you think?"

"It is a mighty ship which glides, not over a real ocean but progresses across the sea of time."

"Yes, yes, that's it; and what service does it offer on this sea? Does it not make the crossing from one summer holiday to another?"

"We say 'summer holidays', Mademoiselle; forgive me for correcting you but I am only doing what I was told by Mama Doloré; – yes, you are right; and the vacations at Easter, Christmas, Whitsun and All Saints' Day are the great ship's ports of call. We let ourselves be carried along; we go about our business; and day by day throughout the seasons, the liner presses on almost inaudibly; see: the sky is slipping by."

Joanny had been happy to find that he was of the same mind as the girl; she had an original way of thinking which presupposed a special sensitivity. On parting, they had shaken each other's hand enthusiastically. Affection could soon grow out of the pleasure they had experienced at being together.

This idea and the memory of that leave-taking gave Joanny the courage he needed to return to his daily life again. He would rest his cheek on his exercise book as he painstakingly wrote; occasionally a shiver of delight would run through his body. He felt so pure and gentle that it was as if she had been sitting there at the same desk by his side.

XI

Henceforth, Joanny was to enjoy three hours of brilliance in his day, of such radiance that they were to light up every other hour with a new light. This was between one and two o'clock and between four and six o'clock in the afternoon.

Never had he woken up more joyfully. As the summer progressed, dawn appeared an hour at least before the drum roll signalled it was time to rise. Awake before everyone else, Joanny would watch the day broaden; still drowsy, his ideas in a jumble, he felt a happiness deep within him, in some part of him, though where exactly he could not say; then he would ask himself why life was so wonderful and, fully awake, he would realize: "Fermina Márquez is the reason."

It was because he was going to see *La Chica* that life was so wonderful. Lying in bed, he viewed things as one does at the start of a convalescence. The windows above all were splendid; vast, curtainless, with their slender iron frames, they entirely encompassed the daybreak. The mist had been, as it were, enclosed, and beyond there were layers of soft blue, of silvery blue, more beautiful than the azure in First Communion pictures of which this colour sky made him think.

Joanny especially remembered one of the pictures he had seen in the country, in a little girl's mass book. On the back there was a prayer by Henri Perreyve to the Virgin; and in this prayer could be read: "Take pity on those who used to love each other and have been parted . . . Pity the heart's isolation." The heart's isolation? Now, Joanny understood what that could be; his egoism was disarmed and he felt like telling Fermina all his secrets and all his hopes.

After a while he could no longer stay lying down like this; he got up quietly, went over to the washbasin, came back, dressed; and as he was ready even before the drum roll reverberated, he remained sitting at the foot of his bed, facing the marvellous windows which were, he did not doubt, less splendid than his own future.

Then, divided up by classes and in rows, we would go for a walk; it was a quarter of an hour in which we covered the walkways of the grounds – the grounds which night had just relinquished and which, fresh and imposing, now threw open their majestic avenues to the sun after awaiting the day in silence. We drank in the air as one might a cold, sweetened drink and when we returned to our studies, we would fill every passage with the scent of the leaves and the dew with which we were imbued.

An unparalleled level of activity swept Joanny through all the physical exercises and morning classes. And from the summons to the dining-hall onwards, his heart would begin to beat for joy and impatience. Finally, on leaving the refectory, he would feign an indifferent air for others and, without hurrying, he would enter the grounds and join Fermina Márquez on the terrace. Here they stayed, strolling at an uneven pace, or they would sit down on a wooden bench standing against a privet hedge. Nobody was able to see them there. And Joanny was extremely anxious not to flaunt the exceptional privilege which Mama Doloré had procured for him in front of his fellow pupils. It was blatantly preferential treatment. But he knew how to mitigate the damaging effect it had had on those he now called "his rivals"; he announced to a group in which Santos, Demoisel, Ortega and a few others were to be found:

"Fermina Márquez sends you her regards and hopes that the

games of tennis can start again soon."

He himself had asked her whether she had anything for him to relay to the gang. He wanted to put all his cards on the table. He had said to himself that the day he obtained a token of undoubted affection, then, at that point but not before, he would walk past all his companions congregated in the yard, by her side. At the moment however, those plans of seduction seemed so far away! It was like that theory about honest women and women of easy virtue: my God, what childishness! He was ashamed of this now. What was the good of philosophizing and of trying to make himself attractive in a systematic way, when each day was bringing him his stock of happiness? When each day he would hear that low and impassioned voice, just a little foreign sounding, with which his own would mingle without constraint and in delight, like breathing.

At two o'clock he returned to his own studies and at three he attended classes. During this time, Mama Doloré and her nieces went for a drive. Having conveyed them from Paris, their victoria used in fact to await them in front of the school gates. They would travel by this means as far as Sceaux and Clamart or to Robinson, where they took tea several times amongst the massive trees. And at four o'clock precisely, they were back at Saint Augustine's.

The Creole lady always had a basket full of sweetmeats for her nephew, who was ruining his teeth by sucking sweets or eating cakes which were too sugary. As only Joanny remained to be looked after, every day she brought a sort of travelling kitchen. This was a small trunk in fine leather, lined with silvered metal; it contained a stove, a silver teapot, a chocolate pot, silver cups with their saucers, spoons, porcelain bowls for sandwiches and butter, caddies for sugar, chocolate and tea, embroidered napkins, a large, flat bottle for milk. It contained such an array of things, you might have thought it was a conjuror's box. All that would be spread out on a bench, and Pilar with Mama Doloré and young Márquez, helped by the footman, would get tea ready, while Joanny and *La Chica* stayed on the terrace. They only came when they were called, hungrily ate what had been prepared for them and returned to the seclusion where they were coming to know each other.

Her manner of speaking always had a certain self-control, a reticence, as if some lofty thought lay behind everything she uttered, as if she related her entire life to this exalted notion. Joanny said to her:

"You make me think of Cervantes' *Espagnole Anglaise*; you know where he says that she was remarkable '*por su hermosura y por su recato*'."

He stammered these words out rather than articulating them. It was the first compliment he had paid her; then he was afraid that she would make fun of his Spanish pronunciation; finally, wasn't there something pedantic, something so hopelessly like a schoolboy in the way he had shown off about his reading?

What astonished Joanny even more was the insistence she would display in talking of humility and in denouncing pride as an especially hideous sin.

"How can you, who are so beautiful, speak of self-abasement?" He had said this quite naturally: the initial flattery had paved the way. But she turned pale and muttered with vehemence: "What, I who am no better than dirt!"

Joanny maintained an embarrassed though respectful silence. He was deeply sensitive, and expressions of immoderation never made him smile . . .

They went on an expedition. He took her on a visit of the classrooms, prep rooms and dormitories. He said to her:

"Look, here's where I sit for prep."

She glanced at the grimy walls, the bare floor covered with stains, the desk on the rostrum, the blackboard. It was so strange to see her there in her gorgeous, light-coloured dress and her wide-brimmed summer hat! He plucked up courage to say: "Sit down in my place; see how hard the bench is and how the desk . . . "

He wanted to express this idea that the desk, by jutting out too much, constrained the pupil's chest; but he could not find any appropriate and seemly way to say it. She had sat down at his place. How good it would feel to work there from now on!

He took her to dormitory La Pérouse, which was his own. As she entered, she crossed herself because of the· crucifix hanging on the wall. Cautiously, she moved across the overly polished tile floor. Joanny, blushing foolishly (he could have kicked himself for vexation), said to her:

"Here is my bed."

She stood a little away from the beds, taking in the dormitory as a whole rather than any spot in particular.

"Our beds are terribly narrow and jolly hard," Joanny added.

She motioned to the crucifix with her finger:

"Remember that for a deathbed the cross was much narrower and harder!"

Dumbfounded, Joanny looked at her. He felt he was really beginning to understand her. Yet how differently they thought. He, for his part, was reflecting how piquant it was that she should be in the middle of the boys' dormitory; and she, at the same moment, was abandoning herself to the transports of a mystical passion.

They went downstairs in silence; and encountering the grounds' freshness once again, they breathed more freely.

Pilar, having caught sight of them, called them.

"What have you got for tea?" asked Fermina in her steady, unconcerned voice.

Pilar imitated the action of a spatula in her hands stirring a chocolate pot.

As they were drawing closer, Mama Doloré asked them where they had been. And on their reply, she became annoyed. While she was talking, her anger mounted. Her reproaches followed one another so quickly that Joanny could no longer make out the words. She concluded her harangue abruptly by standing up and slapping Fermina in the face. The girl caught hold of her aunt's hand, this hand which had just struck her and kissed it reverentially. Joanny, taken aback, was rendered speechless. And what about the footman who had witnessed this domestic scene?

Fermina took the cup of chocolate which her sister was holding out to her. The cheek which her aunt had bruised became quite livid, and the other remained a ghastly pale. Joanny would have liked to throw himself at her feet and cover the hem of her dress with kisses; or considering that his presence could only make her humiliation worse for the girl, he longed to disappear. Soon however, she said in a barely altered voice:

"Pilarcita, do let Mr Léniot have a little napkin."

Trembling all over, his nerves jangling, Joanny had indeed just spilt chocolate on his waistcoat.

XII

The next day he asked her:

"You are very devout, aren't you?"

She hesitated, then said to him:

"Do you mind, but let's not talk about that."

But she came back to the subject of her own accord. The walkways of the grounds had names: avenue La Pérouse, avenue Sibour, avenue Bixiou; these names were painted on metal plaques, nailed here and there to the trees.

"Are these the names of former pupils of Saint Augustine's?"

"Yes"; and he told her what he knew of them. She was full of admiration for Archbishop Sibour.

"He died for truth," she said with fervour.

"No, it's a tale of revenge. Verger, his murderer, was a defrocked priest and half mad.

"You speak of all this so coldly; are you not a believer then?"

Of course he believed; but not in the same way as she. So she realized that her duty was to rekindle the zeal of this Christian, who was so lukewarm. She spoke, she gave free rein to her exaltation. Thus had she come eventually to think only of the Saviour, even when talking about unimportant or frivolous matters. And even in sleep she could feel His presence within her.

"And all my thoughts are His to dispose of; I feel my life is in His dreadful hands and I have to humble myself, wholly purify myself through Communion so that He does not cast me off, repelled by the stench of my sins!"

She would gladly welcome ill health and disease which cleansed her, she thought. Her love and respect for poor people were so great that she would have liked to be able to kneel before them in the roadway. She wished she could be as them. These elegant dresses, all this worldly vanity were burdensome to her; she transformed them into instruments of mortification, for she only wore them to obey her aunt who exercised a mother's authority over her. Occasionally even, she thought she resembled the poor so closely that it seemed to her that she was walking along clothed in rags. Yet was not this very idea prideful? One day, when they had gone out on foot, somebody in a shop had said to them: "No doubt you can't afford it." Mama Doloré had kicked up a fuss and had left furious. But as for her, how happy she had been!

"Just think, we had been taken for poor people!" He asked her whether she gave many alms.

"You well know that these are never matters for discussion; the money we bring the poor, these are trysts we keep with their Father, the King of Heaven."

Joanny looked at this Christian in astonishment; slightly uneasily as well: wasn't there something irreverent in this chatting about matters sacred, in these words spoken in such a manner, out in the open air, in a place and in circumstances which were wholly secular? The religious instruction we received at Saint Augustine's seemed to ignore these transports of ecstasy. We were carefully kept away from theology and mysticism. Our chaplain, formerly with the army, looked more like an old nobleman and soldier than a priest. Sunday mass and vespers also had something military about them: we attended in dress uniform and the servants, in their best livery, were mixed in with us. The result for most of us was that religion was associated with feelings of discipline and decorum. It was an infallible guide when conscience wavered; through it, we could abandon ourselves to Providence; it was a great and shining hope. And we revered it all the more because we did not talk about it.

"You do surprise me," murmured Joanny.

"Perhaps you think that it's the desire for a reward that attracts me to my God? Yet how can one see Him on His Cross and not love Him; love Him for Himself without hope of resurrection and salvation? But to love Him is also to trust in Him, it is to be ready for Him at any time!"

Joanny, while listening to her, thought he was seeing the reverse side of life. Earthly joys, wealth, fame itself became contemptible and unbearable. She stirred up so many ideas in him that he did not resent her for disparaging things he valued most. He heard a jumbled panegyric of Saint Rose of Lima, whom she said she was striving to resemble; and she told him that she would have liked to endure all the agonies of the Cross. One day when she was really thirsty, she had followed her aunt and sister into a boulevard café. They had ordered iced drinks. And at the moment she put her glass to her lips, she had reflected that He had been thirsty in His death throes, and this thought was so appalling that the thirst she herself was experiencing seemed to be full of delight to her; and she had given her glass to Pilar without touching it . . .

She was saying all this in a muffled, breathless voice. Joanny listened without interrupting her. This was her life's secret which she was unveiling to him. After such confidences, could she forget him? She did not display so little constraint with Mama Doloré. She seemed rather to regard her as a tyrannical and capricious mother God had bestowed upon her to try her patience. And Pilar was most certainly not her sister's confidante. Well then? Well, was he not then her friend?

When they took their leave of each other that evening, they shook hands more firmly and for longer than usual. This was a tacit promise to keep their secrets. She said that she would bring him a *Life of Saint Rose of Lima* the next day.

Léniot arrived a little late for prep for the first time. All the pupils were already working. Walking past the sixth-form room, through the half-open door he saw Santos standing by the blackboard which he was covering with equations. "He can have hardly any idea that he has played tennis with a saint!" This thought made Joanny smile. So he was alone in knowing that beneath this gaiety, this flirtatiousness itself, there was such an intense faith, such scorn for the world and riches.

XIII

They had a further conversation, in which they talked of Christian love. Then he read the *Life of Saint Rose of Lima*. Never would this girl who proposed to model her life on such a person, be able to love a man. What a disillusionment! Yet when he placed this book, which she must so often have leafed through, amongst his own in his desk, he was pleased to have at least this one thing of hers.

"Poor little thing," he said to himself as a fresh idea had just flashed through his mind, "poor little thing, if *they* had heard you speaking in this way, how they would have made fun of you!" *They* were the young ladies from his region, the ones who had made him suffer so with their mocking remarks. For stupidity is dreadful in this one respect, that it can resemble the deepest wisdom. When it opens its mouth, it gives itself away immediately; but where it remains hidden, where it resembles wisdom, is when it merely laughs. These girls were "very religious and well brought-up"; intellectually, they were the products of eminently right-thinking boarding schools; and anything which struck them as extraordinary without nevertheless frightening them, seemed absurd to them at the same time. They would whisper, their looks were always hinting at something, they had pursed smiles and as for their laughter, it was of that appalling, thoughtless sort which greets all the noble and lofty ideas of young, over-enthusiastic schoolboys. Their piety of the "properly brought-up" young lady, proud of the dowries they were to have, was so far beneath that impassioned holiness which lit up the young South American girl's features! Ah! How he despised them and how he was beginning to love Fermina Márquez at the thought alone that her spiritual grandeur could be derided by these "eligible matches" from the provinces. Now he was sure he was in love with her – without hope of course; but naturally forever too.

He acknowledged his defeat: he had thought to win her love and it was he who had fallen enamoured. What he dreaded most of all had occurred. Above all he was surprised that his work did not suffer from this. Far from growing slack or from permitting himself to be distracted, he was in fact working harder than ever. He had formed the habit of supposing her always present at his side. At first, it had simply been a game, of his imagination; he would have reddened to disclose this childishness to anyone. Now it was almost an hallucination. The timbre of her voice had become so familiar to him that he thought he heard it in her absence. Wasn't that the rustling of her dress? Wasn't that the weight of her beloved body settling on the bench? Her body . . . he did not like to think about it. It would have been a desecration. Just as the rest of us live in our guardian angel's presence, so did he in hers. Thus, when meeting her every day in the grounds, he felt as if he had left her only a few moments before. He would have liked to say to her: "It is for you that I work; for you and while thinking of you. And if my desire is to carry off all the prizes in my form, it is to have a little fame to present to you; it is because he whom you have chosen to confide in, can't not be the first among men!"

XIV

"Yes of course I believe; but not in the same way as you. Haven't I told you this already?"

Joanny felt that he had to share his most secret thoughts with her in his turn. For a long time, he had been wanting to tell them to somebody. From an early age, he had abandoned any disclosure of his heart to his parents. Our parents are not made for our emotional revelations. For them, we are simply heirs apparent. They demand only two things of us: firstly, that we take advantage of the sacrifices they make; and then, that we allow ourselves to be shaped as they please, in other words that we become men without delay, so as to take over their affairs; sensible men who will not squander their fortunes acquired at such cost. "Ah, dear parents! We may perhaps grow to manhood; but we will never be sensible." We say that until the age of twenty because we believe we are destined for greatness.

Besides, Joanny's parents had betrayed his trust. The stories he had recounted to them in the initial instances of his homecoming from school — for example, the one about the deserted classroom where cigarettes were smoked in secret and the one where a bottle of champagne had been brought to the sixth-form boys by a servant — they had all been mysteriously reported to the prefect of studies. When the idea that his father was the sneak had crossed his mind, Joanny had felt a sudden shame: the sweetest of ties hitherto binding him to his folks had just snapped. From that moment on, he confided nothing to them any longer. As for them, they did not notice this change: the boy had good marks for his conduct and his work. What more could they ask for?

Above all, the secrets Joanny had to impart were not such as any person whosoever is able to hear. They were grand, sublime thoughts, intended to regenerate the world. Now the serious-minded middle classes, those who work, do not care for abstract politics, pure ideas, utopias. They do not lose sight of material interests. Joanny was aware of a contrast between his parents' opinions and his own dreams which was distressing, almost absurd. And besides, Joanny Léniot's great notion would have made all straightforward people smile. He advocated a return to the hegemony of the Roman Empire, as it existed under Constantine and Theodosius.

We read Victor Duruy reluctantly and it was our loss. For if Duruy's *History of Rome* does not abound in enthusiasm, at least it was supposed to in us. At an age when we were starting to gorge ourselves on Emile Zola and Paul Bourget, sheltered behind our desks, Joanny Léniot was becoming intoxicated by Roman history. The mythical era, the monarchy and the beginnings of the Republic mattered little to him. It was from the Third Punic War that it became truly interesting. But the civilized world, once settled in the Pax Romana, presented a yet more admirable spectacle. Finally, the founding of a line of emperors had crowned off the work.

Oh! Why had the Empire not been better able to assimilate the Barbarians? Why all those little kingdoms? Doubtless, Clovis was raised to the consular purple; was he any less the King of the Francs for this? It was true that the Church lived on powerful and respected, as if the Empire, by dint of being divine, had merged with it – the Church becoming a spiritual Empire. And still to this day, the Church was what was left of the Empire.

"Yes I revere this residue of the Empire, I am hopelessly

caught up in it," Joanny was explaining to his new friend. "Why did Charlemagne allow the division of the Empire? Why didn't Charles the Fifth reconquer the Gauls? Why didn't Napoleon have himself crowned Western Emperor? What is this name of a barbarian tribe which is attached to me: the French? I am not French. My catechism tells me that I am Roman Catholic and I construe that in this way: a Roman and ruler of the world! My sovereign, my only master is this great, lean old man always depicted in white vestments, the divine and august Leo, Emperor of the West! I have seen him; I so implored my parents that they took me to Rome last Easter holidays. We obtained an audience; I spoke to him. I had to say: 'Yes, Holy Father; no, Holy Father' but in my heart of hearts, I was crying out: Caesar!"

"Whereas he himself in his humility only wanted to be called the servant of God's servants!"

"Yes, you believe I'm a heathen. I can quite see it. You think I worship God, not because He is He who is, but because He is the God of Rome. But the God of Rome, the one who has taken the place of Jupiter Capitolinus, might he not be the true God? If only you knew how close to the heavens Rome appears, seen from the Pincio! . . . You cannot imagine what I feel during mass."

Joanny fell silent, breathless. These were no longer secrets now; this was a passionate appeal. In the fervour of his enthusiasm, he had no doubt that he would sweep his interlocutor's opinion along with him.

"When I look at the altar, it isn't lighted candles, covers and flowers of gold but the majesty of Rome that I see. The priest, the faithful are all gathered together there as Roman Catholics; you might as well say as Romans, don't you think? The City is in the hands of infidels; the imperial gods are insulted every day; and yet those in that house glory in being called Romans. O shades of Cato, these are the last citizens! . . . There in that house of the Lord, I hear the language of my true country still spoken: Latin. For your Castillian and our

French and Italian as well are simply dialects stemming from spoken Latin," continued Joanny, reciting his grammar despite himself; "These are vulgar tongues, old peasant patois. A time will come I tell you, when Latin, classical Latin will once again be taught in all the schools of the Empire and when all the vulgar languages will be forgotten. And this day is possibly not so far away as may be supposed . . .

"Do you mind my saying something to you, Mademoiselle? You won't repeat this to anybody though, you promise me? Well then, I have learnt to pronounce Latin all by myself, more or less as the ancient Romans did. It took me a long time. In the first place, because I was unable to practise out loud; in French schools, Latin is pronounced according to certain rules and if there is any departure from them, the other pupils laugh and besides, the masters are not keen on it. When the South Americans are new here, they pronounce Latin in the Spanish manner; but they are very quickly taught to articulate it as the French do. It's not just a question of certain letters; it is also a matter of the number of vowels. It is because I thoroughly grasped this that I am good at Latin verse. Sometimes when I am alone and above all while on country walks during the holidays, I recite long extracts from Lucretius, Virgil and Ovid to myself, stressing the words in the Roman style. You cannot know what pleasure this gives me. I feel that I am conversing with all these great men of antiquity in their own tongue and that they understand me! My misfortune is that I have to watch myself closely when reciting my lessons and reading out the texts of the unseen translations; I have no wish to be noticed for an accentuation which is different from everybody else's . . .

"Mademoiselle, I hope at least I'm not boring you?"

"No, you're not boring me," she replied. And with a sigh she added: "Mr Léniot, why don't you make better use of the gifts which God has bestowed upon you?"

"Fancy that, she has spotted that I am gifted," mused Joanny, gratified.

He carried on: "The whole problem stemmed from the splitting up of the Empire. The number of inhabitants had increased, I admit. Yet two empires, one in the east, the other in the west, or rather one Empire but which like Janus presented the two faces of the civilized world to the barbarism of the universe, were quite enough. Why were usurpers allowed to assume the titles of King of England, Duke of Burgundy, King of France? No, no, we are on imperial ground wherever there sounds Romanic speech: survey the Gauls all around us in the fullness of their summer; see Lutetia yonder. Of course Lutetia of the Parisians has grown since the days when the Emperor Julian would come to spend the winter months there — no it was before he became emperor. The Empire's population has expanded: more state servants will be needed than in days gone by, that is all. There are also the Americas, Australia, the European colonies in Africa. But an administration which has governed half the Empire will surely be able to govern half the world. — At least you don't think what I'm saying is laughable?"

She was listening to him with no lack of interest.

"It's just that on the one or two occasions I have spoken about it, I have been made fun of. My guardian in Paris, one Sunday, first listened to me without saying anything, then advised me to read a novel by Flaubert, *Bouvard et Pécuchet*, in order to find 'my kind' of idea. I clearly understood from his tone that he meant this in jest, and I have no desire to read these modern books, written by authors who would perhaps be incapable of translating their own works into good Latin! . . . On another occasion, I wanted to explain my views to an old family friend, who struck me as more intelligent than the rest of the gathering. He started to laugh immediately and told me that he had run across many reactionaries in his life but never a man as reactionary as myself, and that it was not good for the son of an old republican to have such ideas. You see in the interior, or as we say, in the provinces, the children are obliged to have the same political opinions as their parents: if they don't, they are shown little regard. Ah! mademoiselle, you cannot imagine how backward the interior still is! Anyway, this man was laughing. So, to annoy him, I told him that I saw myself not so much as a Frenchman but as a Roman citizen. I had surmised correctly: that put him into a temper straight away. I had disturbed his pathetic grubs of ideas and they writhed about in his cramped skull. He was completely red. How small, how petty-minded he seemed to me; I had him in my hand; there he twitched like an insect being tormented. I saw in him not so much a man as a manufactured product, a machine which talks and thinks in the approved manner. Ah! If ever I felt superior to somebody else, it really was to that imbecile!"

"Oh! Mr Léniot, it isn't right to speak in such a manner!"

There was such a note of reproach in the girl's voice that Joanny fell silent, wholly discomposed. Up until that point, he had held forth with the unshakable self-assurance given by the certainty of commanding his listener's whole-hearted approval. Yet, which was quite the reverse, here she was remonstrating against what he had said, at the end of her patience. In short then, he had displeased her; and this was the worst thing which could have befallen him. He continued to speak but his heart was no longer in his words. Everything he was preparing to give brilliant expression to a moment before, suddenly appeared ludicrous, hollow and without interest. He embarked upon a digression and broached the subject of Roman virtues. He exalted poverty especially:

"Rome," he said, "is Need's eldest daughter: herein lies the secret of her power. The poets of the Augustan era were conscious of this themselves. Listen to what Horace says:

"*Hunc* . . . This word refers to Fabricius of whom he has just spoken.

Hunc et incomptis Curium capillis,
Utilem bello tulit, et Camillum
Saeva paupertas et avitus arto
Cum lare fundus!

"*Saeva paupertas:* cruel destitution" . . .

Joanny was struck dumb; he had just read in the girl's eyes a thought which threw him into turmoil. These eyes seemed to say: "Does he mean to be insolent? Is he making fun of me?" Then he remembered that a lady to whom he had declaimed a passage from Tacitus one day, had said to him in an angry tone of voice: "If you want to insult me, just go ahead. I don't have any idea what you're talking about."

The call to evening prep parted them straight away. She did not hold out her hand to him . . .

Throughout the evening, Joanny felt a throbbing in his temples and his cheeks were on fire. He had displeased her. He had been ridiculous at first; and then odious! Ah! those long, idiotic and childish tirades: "Leo, Emperor of the West" and the invocation to the shades of Cato! There was enough in this to die of shame. He would have liked to disavow these phrases. At least if he had written them, he could have erased them with a rubber. But there is no rubber in the world that can erase in other people's memories what we have said to them. He ought to have apologized for that Latin quotation as well. But what must have shocked her deeply was the disparagement of his fellow citizens and the repudiation of his country.

"This must seem monstrous to that poor girl! There can be nothing more conservative than a woman; her ideas are always a generation behind the times at least!"

When he had jeered at the crassness of the provincial republican from the pinnacle of his intellect, how her sense of decency, her loathsome, insulted sense of decency had quivered within her! What, she was the same on all counts as the "manufactured product" who had excited his anger. Then he regretted he had not shocked her more, had not goaded her to snapping point. It was a game: with a few well-chosen paradoxes you could scourge the wits of fools: first of all, they lost their tempers and then they ended up by howling like dogs. Oh! What pleasant little parlour games!

A fool? But what was meant by that? Did this distinction he

64

drew so clearly correspond with reality? It was truly an oversimplification to say that there were two types of people: those without and those with brains, and naturally to number oneself amongst the latter! And yet classical poets considered it a virtue to hold the vulgar herd in contempt. Ah! He was tired of these reflections. The truth was that there were certain things which were not for anybody's ears. Just as one did not take exceptional pains to dress up to go into town, because of the street urchins' chorus of shrieks, so the unusual thoughts one had should not be revealed to anybody whomsoever: one might hear the words: "Oh! Mr Léniot, it isn't right to speak in such a manner."

And he who thought he had found, if not a lover, at least a friend, a companion to whom there would be nothing he could not say, an equal! *An equal!* – fine! He was once again sinking back into his theories about human stupidity. He had displeased her and that was all there was to it.

On the next day he apologized the best he could: "Yesterday evening I distressed you deeply with my paradoxes and I was so ill-mannered as to quote Latin. Admit that I really bored you?"

"No, not at all. I do assure you; and you didn't *distress* me the least bit."

"You are very kind to say that to me. But from now on, we shall be good friends shan't we? . . . I would so much like you to remember things favourably."

She said nothing in reply. He felt a long way away from her, altogether alien to her life. But this impression soon passed.

They never again alluded to this incident.

XV

A few days afterwards he returned *The Life of Saint Rose of Lima* to her. In this book he had come across several of the most vivid expressions which she had used in their conversations, for example, "the Cross's narrow and hard bed". He could have mentioned this to her but he was afraid he would upset her too much. Assuming despite himself an air of self-importance, he contented himself by saying: "It's an old Spanish translation of the Acts of the Saints. Its Castillian is redolent of the end of the Golden Age."

"You know about Spanish literature as well? You are a true scholar Mr Léniot . . . "

"Oh! Mademoiselle . . . "

She was not poking fun at him; she had even endeavoured to invest her question with a tone of respect. Joanny was puffed up with pride.

"Yes really: Mr Santos Iturria said one day in my presence that you were the best pupil in the school."

So he tried to explain the grading of the prepared work, the compositions, the roll of honour to her. But in this he was overeager and it was immediately plain that he attached too much importance to it. Outside school, all that meant nothing whatsoever, was indeed hardly possible to understand. He fell silent as if forbidden to speak; he no longer dared utter the word "composition", which suddenly struck him as conveying a childish notion which would amuse adults not without justification. He felt that their want of intellectual maturity stood revealed in everything they said, in the way she had expressed her religious sentiments as in the way he had spoken to her about Roman history.

"You work hard?" she said.

"Yes I do, very. People think that I learn without difficulty but it isn't true; I am not quick-witted, I don't grasp things straight away. You see, I even admit my imperfections to you."

She asked him whether he exerted himself so strenuously out of inclination for his studies or rather out of obedience to his parents.

"No, it is to find favour in someone's eyes; to be worthy of somebody . . . a month ago, I did not know exactly whom I wished to please but I knew that this person would appear. It was to honour her coming that I decorated my whole life with glory, that I made of it a splendid palace where she would come to dwell. Now this person has arrived . . . it's you."

So there it was, he had said it. She did not blush; she remained composed. She was so beautiful he thought he felt the warmth of her face. After a while, she asked which class Santos Iturria was in. Then her conversation was purely of unimportant matters. They parted from each other earlier than they normally did.

Unforeseen, almost unnoticed, the great moment had arrived, had gone past – in profound silence. It was a complete failure this time. Joanny was furious that he had lied to no avail. For in the end, it was not for Fermina Márquez' wonderful eyes – admittedly deeply wonderful – that he was working. This had to happen: he now detested her, that holier-than-thou bigot!

On the next and following days up until the Whitsun holidays, they constantly stayed in Mama Doloré's company, exchanging no more than social niceties.

XVI

Camille Moûtier was a second-form pupil. At thirteen, he was a whey-faced little boy, with brown hair which was always too severely cropped and doleful eyes. You could guess that the looks he gave had been full of life and mischievous but in days gone by before he entered the school. For he was not suited to school life. For him, it was a torture which was revived every day. You would see from observing him he had so assumed the habit of suffering that it had become his closest friend.

His unique aspiration was to make himself invisible, to disappear. He experienced the distress which masters, a blinkered administration, can impose through their reprimands and punishments. And he knew too of the anguish inflicted by the others, his brutal companions, those above all who are well versed in the torture of a soul through fearful sarcasm or through humiliations which make death desirable. He had already even thought several times of doing away with himself; but religious qualms had prevented him from this. So he resigned himself to living. Indeed, he even tried to give an impression of jauntiness so as not to bring further persecution upon himself by his woebegone air. Occasionally, almost unable to check his desire to cry any longer at roll call or in the dining hall for example, he would start pulling faces, at which everyone laughed but which would help him to force back his tears.

Camille Moûtier had quickly become a very bad pupil. The punishments and the black marks were in fact much easier to endure than the thousand and one taunts of his companions. At the beginning, he had fought stoutheartedly and even now he succeeded in striking a few blows when the relics of anger were rekindled in him. But his rage had been consumed by despair. His tormentors hounded him relentlessly. And furthermore, his pride was of such a delicate nature that certain jokes which others would have put up with in good part and which can be stopped by retaliating once and for all, affected him like serious affronts whose memory tortured him. Dear Lord, we can't be good.

He would wait for night to weep without constraint. If you have not been made an apple-pie bed and if a plate full of purée has not been slipped between your two sheets, you can sob your heart out. Camille bided his time until everybody was asleep; then all his sorrow welled up in his eyes, spilled over and trickled down his cheeks. I have listened to this vast despair of a child: sobs can't be heard, nothing can be except an *imperceptible snivelling* at long intervals. If the monitor were awake, he might think that some hoaxer was whistling.

So the joy which holidays brought little Moûtier was almost too great for him. Those holidays! He relished their every minute, they were trysts with himself; he rediscovered himself, unrestrained and gay as he had been before going to school. For a few days or weeks, he ceased to be a suffering, sobbing wretch. And his parents seeing him so gladsome, so absorbed in his games, with so much of the child about him, were disarmed by the insouciance, the unalloyed happiness of childhood; of childhood such as Madame Amable Tastu and Victor Hugo have celebrated it: the best time of life.

But the appearance of Fermina Márquez in the existence of the school stripped his holidays of much of their fine flavour for little Camille Moûtier. Now he had found something to love in his place of torment. From the first minute, he was certain that he would never dare step up to her, that he would never mean anything to her. Before he had even attracted her attention, he used to pray for her every night. He was jealous of Santos and he was jealous of Léniot. In his thoughts, he gave himself to her forever, blind to everything else around him, deaf, enraptured.

He came back to life once again. Several fights in which he had had the best of it had kept his bullies at bay for a little while. So he nerved himself to make friends with young Márquez who was in the second form as well. He was pleased to be seen around with Márquez: wasn't he by this means much closer to her; wasn't his name associated with hers in the minds of those who saw him walking at Márquez' side? The names of those who became inseparable were written up on the walls; over-exclusive friendships were ridiculed and underwent such persecution that sometimes they were successfully broken up. Well, the day Camille Moûtier read on the riding school's walls the inscription: "Moûtier and Márquez", he was more elated than he had ever been since his arrival at Saint Augustine's: "If only she had read that!"

He would bring all his talk around to her: to speak of her brother was also to speak of her; to speak of Paris where she was living; to speak of Colombia, South America, Spain's history, the Battle of Rocroi was to speak of her as well. The progress he made in Castillian was astounding: was not Castillian Fermina Márquez' mother tongue? And in this strange Christian name: Fermina, he saw something wonderful; for him it epitomized all earthly beauty. It was the finest word man had uttered. He would never have found the courage to say it out loud: Ferminita. This diminutive was too familiar, too close to her.

Yet if he had just had a chance to be glimpsed by her . . . just glimpsed! . . . At Whitsun, he had the luck to spend the whole day in Paris; not one of those sullen, dismal Sundays, when all the shops have deliberately shut to stop schoolboys and cadets from Saint Cyr's taking a look, but a proper, bustling Paris day. The Saint Cyr boys for their part seem to smile mysteriously as they walk past the closed shop fronts: they have seen the window displays the previous Thursday. But for schoolboys, no window shopping: they might forget their compositions as a result. This goes for bookshops too which do not exist as far as they are concerned: they have to make do with editions of the classics; and contemporary literature is not for them. Besides, it is worthless: the chief monitors who furnish themselves with libraries from the pupils' confiscated novels would have you believe that to begin to show any talent, an author must be in his grave for seventy-five years.

Camille Moûtier had spent an entire Saturday in Paris at the house of his guardian who having recalled the existence of the little schoolboy, had his manservant collect him from Saint Augustine's. It was a chore for the manservant: he had to put up a pretence of listening to everything this small boy told him of South America and the glories of the Castillian language. Once he had arrived at the gloomy flat in the rue des Saints-Pères, Camille Moûtier was immediately entrusted to a nephew of his guardian, a young man aged twenty who was studying law.

Camille had already come across him, this grown-up law student; but he would not have been able to say where or when. This apartment and this family always struck him like objects and people seen in a dream, a dream which sometimes recurs but which never lasts long enough for a place's look and people's features to be engraved on the sleeper's memory. Even the notion of their ties of kinship was uncertain for him; was this elderly lady a regular Sunday guest, an aunt from the provinces or his guardian's mother? He mistook each one of them for the other. He was only sure of recognizing his guardian himself: he would always wear a frock coat with silk lapels and a skullcap of black velvet.

He could ignore them with impunity; for their part, they did not put themselves out for him: they continued their daily existence in front of him, speaking of affairs and people he was not acquainted with. It was a dream, neither good nor bad; rather it was wearisome, for although he was careful to avoid becoming involved in the concerns of the parties, he was obliged to watch his behaviour and reply to their enquiries. At table, for instance, you never knew if it were really you who was being asked a question.

Thus on this summer's day, beneath the streets' sky newly painted blue, Camille Moûtier dreamt he was out walking with Gustave, the phantom who was studying law. Gustave felt somewhat ashamed to be seen with a schoolboy. And any conversation with this kid struck him as impossible: they had nothing in common. It was a wasted day. Yet what did it matter! He would recoup many other summer days which would make up for this one; other days spent in infinitely more interesting company. He responded monosyllabically to Camille Moûtier who was offering him profuse explanations of the discovery of the Darien, the expedition of Balboa and how New Grenada had become Colombia. This little boy was well up in his geography. A few moments later, his voice quavered terribly and Gustave, who was not even thinking of him any more, had pricked up his ears: the little boy was talking about one of his companions called Francisco Márquez and this companion's sister, Fermina.

"Fermina! That's quite a name to remember! Fermina!" Gustave blasphemed. They stopped in the arcade in front of the wonderful toyshop on the corner of the rue du Louvre and the rue de Rivoli. The little boy as befits little boys, did not grow tired of gazing at the display. They had to enter the shop. And Gustave was surprised to see him buy a miniature flag, a flag printed in silk glued to an iron pole. "What could the little boy want to do with this novelty?" Truly, adults are incapable of understanding anything.

And the day after his return, at the one o'clock break, having noticed Mama Doloré and her nieces in the grounds, Camille Moûtier left the yard, his heart beating very loud: once out of the monitors' sight, he began to run and like a handsome knight arrayed in his lady's colours, he passed in front of Fermina, holding in his hand a small, fluttering replica of the Colombian flag.

"Look," exclaimed the girl, "my national flag!"

Camille Moûtier retraced his steps and stammered: "I was going to take it to Paquito; where is he, Mademoiselle?" He did not even wait for the reply. This was already more than his nerve could endure. He took to his heels.

That was his big adventure that year.

XVII

Santos Iturria appeared radiating well-being on return from
the Whitsun holiday. He never took advantage of a break and
it was some event to hear him being called to the counter of
the visiting room on a leave-out day. He himself seemed not to
set much store by these breaks; his nocturnal outings in the
Negro's company were enough for him. But as that year's
Whitsun holiday drew near, he had put everything in place to
obtain leave. And he had succeeded in having himself invited
by a young secretary at the Mexican legation whom he had
come across in Montmartre.

Joanny Léniot understood himself clearly; he had certainly
said: he was not quick-witted and he did not grasp things
straight away. Even when Santos had said to him after
bumping into him in a passage on the day after our return:
"Léniot you squirt, there are two people you're really
bothering," he hadn't cottoned on. Seeing was the only thing
for it.

And he had seen.

"*La Chica* will be here in a moment," said Mama Doloré
greeting Joanny. He replied with great calmness: "Yes; she is
in the arbour with Iturria major."

"Oh really?" said Mama Doloré without concern.

Pilar gave him in earnest one of her wonderful looks of dark
fervour. Did this girl know? Perhaps she felt sorry for him.

That was all he needed!

"When she returns, tell her that I will be waiting on the terrace."

He stepped up to it. A few minutes later, Fermina Márquez was by his side. He did not say hello. But with a theatrical gesture, he pointed to Paris, that is to say that scant, greyish mist perceptible on the horizon. "It is thanks to my peers that this city is worthy of being called the City of Light. Do you understand?"

She said nothing in reply.

"Do you understand?"

Realizing that she had resolved to remain silent, he turned towards her and spoke the august truth: "Genius breathes in me."

She said nothing. She was expecting a scene of a different sort. She even felt relieved to see events taking this course. As for him, he was looking at her with a composure he had never before commanded in her presence. He was even able to look her in the face without being dazzled. He thought he bore an inner beauty beside which the girl's paled.

"When I told you that it was to appeal to you or a woman that I was working, I lied. I lied and I'm proud of it! I work for myself. I am possessed by so great an ambition that only the safeguard of immortal fame can ever satisfy it. I am really surprised that you didn't understand earlier on that you were dealing with a man of genius."

He gave a nervous laugh; but went on gently straight away: "I know it's possible to be mistaken. Especially with me, who have nothing but my genius and am wholly lacking in *polish* as they say; wholly lacking in sparkle, without conversation and social talents and am almost stupid after all! Yes, I am quite alone with the burden of my genius, which you might compare to a mountain of great height, dark and steep, the appearance of which is too forbidding for you to look at, Mademoiselle. Oh! Hear me out, I won't say anything which might distress you. Come, let us sit down."

He took her by the hand and led her off. She yielded, not even wishing to leave. She knew that he had just seen her in the arbour with Santos. Now, it looked to her as though it was no longer a question of that but of far weightier matters which she scarcely understood.

He pronounced:

"No woman's love will ever be enough to fill my heart. Renown is what I want. And a genuine renown, which has not been demanded. Around me, I see gifted students who are not satisfied by being punctual and doing faultless prepared work; they feel the need to strengthen their positions through all sorts of petty intrigues: they try to be of service to the monitors, they laugh at all the teachers' classroom quips. Such behaviour is impossible for me: my appearance, just like my spirit, is too forbidding. I work without the least display of zeal; but if only you knew how ferociously I apply myself! I pretend to be indifferent to the actual compliments I receive. Finally, I like to feel that all the teachers find me disagreeable, yet despite that, have no alternative but to give me the best marks.

"I have Julien Morot, the novelist, as my guardian in Paris. It seems he is well known. I have such respect for fame that I even think well of his own, which I wouldn't want to have in the least. It's fame like that of a firm: it keeps itself going only through never-ending publicity. Rewarded by services rendered to people of influence, by dinner parties and receptions, by money itself, it is publicity which is at the root of this writer's celebrity. Moreover, he understands fame's worth! He said to me one day: 'You should make connections, it's the only way to succeed.' Do you realize, that means he holds his fame in contempt; for him it's a business which he exploits and which yields him a return of so much a year. He would love to have the time to write for his own pleasure, to be able to release the genius in himself. But he's caught up in the system: publishers, editors of reviews overwhelm him with commissions. He's never left alone. And as for him, he knows that his celebrity is an illusion; that ten years after his death, his name will have slipped into profound oblivion; and that even that celebrity he enjoyed in his lifetime will do him no service in the view of posterity: for once scorn has settled on the works of his maturity, it will also shroud his first two or three books, which so he says, he wrote in innocence, with faith and enthusiasm, his first two or three books which are without question his greatest work. He knows all that. Sometimes I have thought: 'Why doesn't he prefer a modest fortune, obscurity in his lifetime and posthumous glory to this artificial fame and this debasement of his talent?' But one day, he gave me a terrible answer to this question I had asked myself. As I was talking to him about some modern theory of aesthetics: 'Art for art's sake is all very well,' he said; 'but you see, you've got to live.' And he looked at his wife and children; he has even lost the right to be poor.

"As I set out in life, Julien Morot's example clarifies my instincts, by contrast. To my career in politics, I will apply principles which are wholly opposed to those guiding his life as an artist. I won't be dependent on anything or anybody. My isolation will be complete; it already is. I will stay buried in silence and in darkness; I will shun the world. My youth will be like Lieutenant Bonaparte's. I will, if I have to, endure the world's scorn, the sniggering of fools, with patience, I will brave the incredulous smiles of my close relations calmly – but the day my sun rises above it, all humanity will fall to its knees before my morning radiance.

"I'll wait. I am patient. From the moment I had thoughts, sensations, I realized I had genius. So I became accustomed to being misunderstood. My mother would take me to the dressmaker's and the grocer's and to my astonishment, neither of them saw that I was a child prodigy. I shouldn't have been astonished. Even to this day, they don't understand that I am a man of genius; they are unable to see that. They don't even know that I am good at school; or if my mother told them this, they have forgotten it. They greet me obsequiously; but it's because they have been informed that my father earns two hundred thousand francs a year from the silk trade. They honour in me the power of money, which I myself despise. They will only pay tribute to my genius the day they have seen me ride in front of the entire army with a quiet and morose air! I can remember when I was nine, actually when I was seven, the elderly would come to our house. Their lives were done and they were approaching the threshold of death without renown. Without renown; the two terrible words! Had they ever even wanted fame? Did at least the majestic ruins of vast, shattered hopes lurk in their souls? No; they had never had ambition. They had been students in Paris and then came to the provinces to set themselves up as notaries or attorneys. They prided themselves on never having wanted anything fanciful in their existences, in other words anything noble. And as for me, a taciturn little boy, a person of no importance, in my heart I despised them. They had passed through life in silence like animals, hunched over the ground by nature and enslaved by her to their base appetites . . . "

He had a moment's hesitation: "That comes from Sallust," he said; and he carried on: "Yet at that time, I hardly knew what fame was; what ambition was and all these passions which are so strong in me . . . On other occasions, we had to greet and entertain tradesmen, financiers, in short every sort and kind of common person. Since I would never speak to them, because the mere sight of them was enough to sicken me, they took me for a backward child and would ask: 'So what are we called then?' One day, I answered one of them in the most deliberate and mild of ways possible: 'Im-be-cile.' My father slapped me; but I had managed to cause quite a bit of a stir, I assure you.

"Oh Mademoiselle, my modesty and humility are boundless! As long as a man hasn't expressely disowned his own genius in front of me, I believe in it. But nearly all men, with a quite remarkable candour I admit, hasten to repudiate all claims to it. You even run across those who tell you: 'As soon as a person acquires something of the critical faculty, he only has to be intelligent to realize he isn't a genius.' It's in this way that they acknowledge their nonentity; that they inflict this appalling *deminutio capitis* on themselves. I have seen so many give up in this fashion! Mademoiselle, *now* you are able to understand my profession of faith: I despise the critical faculty, I hate science and I only respect human emotions because they alone count amidst all the follies of the modern age!"

He had not stopped looking at her. He was telling her the wildest things; things he would not even have dared admit to himself at any other time. And yet he was dominating her. As for her, she let him ramble on resignedly. There she remained, hardly listening to what he was saying, waiting for him to finish. He went on: "Consider my position a little bit. Am I not like a man possessing billions hidden underground? This fellow lives in a small town he can never leave; this small town where you can't find anything you might call luxury. He is compelled to live like the other inhabitants, without ever being able to spend his billions. And the people of this little village don't want to believe that he really has this fabulous wealth. And when he talks about his billions, they laugh in his face. Have you read *The Secret of Mr Synthesis* by Louis Boussenard? I read it when I was nine and I remember it still. In this book, there is a character who is the richest and most learned man in the world; this is Doctor Synthesis. He has reserves at his disposal which would allow him to become overnight 'the basic proprietor of the earth'. Just let my hour come and I too have, not in banks but within myself, what I need to become the basic proprietor of the earth! And my hour will come. It certainly did for Lieutenant Bonaparte. Doesn't Joanny Léniot have just as fine a ring to it? To flatter my parents, the lesser folk at home readily say to me: 'You will be so rich one of these days, Master Joanny.' They have scarcely any idea how rich I will be in fact. They would die of envy. Would you like a proof of my genius? Well listen to this then.

"A few years ago, my father made me attend the classes of a

primary school in our part of Lyons before sending me to Saint Augustine's. My father, I should say, intended to stand as a candidate for some state post or other. It was to curry favour with the plebs that he made me go to this school. I had to leave it at the end of a month: the pupils — all of them — harassed me and would have ended up by killing me. It was thought that they were jealous of my middle-class way of dressing, my good manners, my father's wealth, finally that they were disgruntled I wasn't like them, in other words a lout. No doubt there was something of all these feelings in their hatred for me; but this loathing was really too intense: they had sensed the man of genius in me and it was the man of genius that these young Gauls were instinctively persecuting.

Men said to each other: 'He is a stranger to us.'

"Ah! The day I pass by the front ranks of their legions once I've mixed them into the vast crucible of my army with all the peoples of the Empire; once I've made Roman citizens of these savage, inland Gauls, with what heartfelt warmth will they cry out: *Ave Caesar!* — and when the grandchildren of their great-grandchildren read my life story in their history books, how they will sob with admiration and love for me!"

He eyed her steadily. He could have continued to bare his soul before her in this manner. He was deriving intense pleasure from this. He had lost his respect for her or at least he was no longer going to put himself out for her. He rose to his feet, wishing to bring the meeting to an end himself.

"I had come to tell you, Mademoiselle, that I will no longer have the pleasure of spending my breaks in your company. I had asked my father's permission to take one or two watercolour lessons before the summer holidays so as to have an outdoor pastime next August and September. My father has given me his permission; I have been to see the drawing master . . . we are to make a start with flowers; it will be very interesting. In short, my afternoon breaks will be employed in the drawing school from now on. I bid you farewell. I will take my leave of your dear aunt and sister . . . Mademoiselle . . . "

He bowed ceremoniously. He was surprised to see that she offered him her hand. And her handshake was remarkably vigorous; she really did *hold* on to his hand.

He immediately went to say goodbye to Mama Doloré, giving the same excuse, trotting out the same lie. "Does she realize that these watercolour lessons are just a pretext?" he wondered – Pilar had unquestionably understood. He thought he saw regret in her parting glance: "I wouldn't have said no." But can one ever tell? "After all, I may have interpreted this look in the wrong way; and surely I have my share of innate self-conceit like everybody else?" reasoned Joanny to himself.

Nevertheless, he went to request a meeting with the prefect of studies. As from the next day, he had to start his watercolour lessons without waiting for his father's authorization which he was already sure of obtaining and which he would write to ask for this very evening. The usher made him wait in the anteroom. He found himself sitting opposite a mirror. As there was nothing inside the school to reflect your face, your own traits soon ceased being familiar to you and you knew your companions' features better than your own. There were a few narcissistic youths who possessed a number of small pocket mirrors which they would use affecting an air of mystery. But Joanny was not one of those; and he became reacquainted with his image in this mirror as one does with a person one knows and whose face one studies at each fresh encounter. It is by observing himself in his looking-glass that a man manages to modify his facial expressions, as much as it is in his power to. Joanny saw some of his customary states of mind written plainly across his features with a surprise mingled with concern. The overwatchful look in his eyes; this crease in his brow; these were what he had to eliminate. Yes, a "severe countenance"; that was indeed what it was. A matt complexion, brown eyes, and above all practically motionless facial muscles, cheeks incapable of breaking into a smile; a heavy, hard face, though delicately drawn, almost classical; *Roman*.

The ring of an electric bell summoned the usher into the office of the prefect of studies. Then the usher returned to announce "pupil Léniot".

Pupil Léniot greeted the prefect of studies. He indicated to him his desire to take lessons in watercolouring; and in a few minutes, everything was settled. Next, he said that since his breaks would be taken up by these lessons in the future, he would no longer be able to accompany "the Márquez ladies" in their walks through the grounds. "It would perhaps be appropriate to name another pupil to take my place with them," he added with a slight intonation of irony which the prefect of studies did not notice at all.

"Indeed; but which pupil?"

"I am sure that they will be only too happy to accept Santos Iturria."

"Good. You will tell Iturria major that I wish to speak to him, that he should come here . . . Ah! Mr Léniot," added the prefect of studies, as Joanny was making for the door. "I can certainly inform you straight away; you have been chosen by the teaching board to deliver the speech in Latin for His Eminence. His Eminence will be honouring us with a visit in a fortnight's time; hold yourself in readiness. I congratulate you in all sincerity and I have no doubt that in this matter you will uphold the school's reputation as well as your own. I shan't detain you any longer."

Prep had already started. Léniot, passing by the sixth-form room, pushed the door open and walked in. He conveyed the prefect of studies' command, summoning Santos Iturria to his office, to the monitor. "So he will realize that it is me who is smoothing the path to their meetings," mused Joanny. He felt no jealousy.

He was even glad. Once he was seated at his place in his prep room and at peace, he enquired into the reasons for his contentment. It was first of all this tremendous piece of news that the prefect of studies had just announced to him: he had been singled out to deliver the speech in Latin for the Archbishop. That was a distinction he had never dared hope for.

"When the others find that out! – And as for my parents!"

But there was something else which he was still more pleased about: this was the oration he had just made to Fermina Márquez. He had improvised it swiftly, as he would his best compositions in French while walking in the yard at break: he would keep them "in his head" for several days, modifying them, touching them up, doing away with an adverb, moving the whole of a phrase around. And an hour before the time set for the scripts to be handed in, he would write out his composition directly as a tidy copy without any crossing-out. So it was that he had been able to recite the entire speech he had made to the girl, breaking off with her, from beginning to end without hesitation. This caused him satisfaction: he was quite sure that this time he had not been ridiculous.

He barely regretted the somewhat quick-tempered words: "Tradesmen, financiers, every sort and kind of common person", and Márquez senior was a banker! But no, this was no foolishness. All the time he had been speaking, Joanny had felt that from the depths of his consciousness, a hidden force was urging him to say this and that it had all been imbued with a significance more full than he had thought. In short, he had lied once again. His genius for example. It was the first time he asserted the existence of his genius to himself. When he read that *Life of Franklin*, he had no faith in his own gifts. When some other pupil's prepared work was read out in class, he would marvel at the thousand and one subleties of thought, the deftness of translation in scores of places which he himself would never have hit upon. Times without number, he had experienced the truth of the feeling expressed by this line:

My astonished genius trembles before his.

There were in fact in his life, for the few moments when it seemed to him that his personality filled the world, days upon days when he would feel reduced to an atom and when the universe was so vast that the idea of his own nothingness would terrify him. About his modesty and humility he had thus been sincere. But again, he had used a device when supplying what he had called a *proof* of his genius. While he was talking about persecution, he had associated the following ideas in a vague way: Jean-Jacques Rousseau – persecution mania – genius. His proof was a twofold one: inductive, in his claim to be persecuted because of his genius; and deductive, because the man of genius often believes he is being persecuted. Oh! What brilliance that was!

In sum, all his eloquence amounted to this: "Between Santos Iturria and me you have made your choice. So be it. But know then whom you have spurned and rue me!" Not for a moment had he thought to reproach her for her flirtatiousness, to tell her how much this coquetry was at variance with her religious talk; in short, to accuse her of hypocrisy. "So that was what she was dreading!" So that was why her farewell had been so warm.

Without pausing, he thought of her little sister's beautiful, solemn eyes, "I wouldn't have said no." He remembered all Pilar's gestures and all her pretty manners. One day when her large ribbon had come undone, he had seen her unadorned hair spread out across her shoulders, absolutely black tresses, which must have been dense and resistant to the touch. Fermina had tied the ribbon up again, taking the locks in handfuls . . . Did they sleep in the same room? . . . "I wouldn't have said no." He retained the memory of this glance as if it had been one of an actual caress which made him redden and wholly electrified his blood.

Almost every Thursday, the sisters of Requena (a little boy in the juniors' penultimate class) came with their mother to spend the afternoon at Saint Augustine's. They were three young girls from Cuba with saucy eyes: Pilar, Encarnacion and

Consuelo, sixteen, fifteen and fourteen years old respectively. Joanny had often heard them talked about and he had occasionally seen them. It was said that they would allow themselves to be kissed in any corner of the grounds. They liked kissing for its own sake and not because of those who were doing the kissing. Consequently, they were not at all jealous and it was possible to make comparisons and determine whether the lips of a sixteen-year-old were softer than those of a fourteen- or fifteen-year-old.

A fifteen-year-old. Joanny noticed that there was something sensual simply in the designations of these ages: fifteen, sixteen, seventeen, etc. Pronounce these words out loud and think of girls . . . As from the start of the next school year, he would find a way to spend Thursday afternoons in the grounds . . . Oh! To subdue a girl of that proud race. They were rumoured to be so caressing, despite all their haughty airs . . . And even if the little Requenas were to come next Thursday . . .

Or again during the holidays; he would no doubt find an opportunity. One day when he had wandered a long way away from his parents' house in the country (it was during the last summer holidays), a young shepherdess, standing in the middle of a field, had hailed him to ask for news of a serving girl at his parents'. And he hadn't understood, the oaf, that this was merely a pretext seized upon by the young peasant girl to make contact with "the little master from the big house". Ah! If a similar opportunity presented itself again, he wouldn't let it pass by. Just so, he was going to be sixteen towards the end of August; it was high time for him to learn a thing or two.

He could remember as well a little maid his parents had had in days gone by. He was scarcely twelve years old at that time. The maid was called Louise and was nineteen. One day, she had pinched a lead soldier from him, a general to which he was particularly attached. She had pretended to conceal this plaything in her blouse between her skin and her chemise, and she had said to Joanny: "If master wants it, he'll have to look for it."

And he had looked for "it", feigning great anger but actually wholly confused and flushed with pleasure . . . Perhaps he was going to find a little maid of that Louise's sort during these holidays at his parents'. She was so neat and so sweet, that Louise. A serving girl? Bah! A girl is always a girl. And if need be, he could reach Régny, the nearest station, by bicycle from his parents' house in the country. By leaving immediately after the midday meal, he would have enough time to spend a whole two hours in Roanne. He would be back for dinner and nobody at home would suspect him of having gone into town. A woman is always a woman whatever clothes she's wearing. Joanny pressed his two hands to his heart; he was losing his head; he was seeing red. He thought he would die.

＊　＊　＊

. . . The dream in which I thought I saw wise Mentor descend to the Elysian Fields ended by disheartening me: a secret and pleasant languor was taking hold of me. I was already enjoying the insinuating poison which slipped from vein to vein and soaked right through to the marrow of my bones. Yet I let out more deep sighs; I shed bitter tears; I roared like a lion in my rage. Oh unhappy youth! I said: oh Gods, you who play cruelly with men, why do you make them pass through that age, which is a time of folly and feverish ardour? Oh! Would that I were covered with white hair, bowed and near my grave like Laertes, my grandfather! Death would be sweeter to me than the shameful weakness in which I find myself.

Throughout the whole of *Telemachus*, Joanny only really liked two passages: the description of the Cretan sages in Book Five and that passage where Telemachus, with the very passion and exaggeration of the young, curses youth. He had wanted to reread this passage. Up until that point, he had admired it, above all because he could see in it a portrayal of what the youth of others amounted to. These frenzies, "this time of folly and feverish ardour", that was what other young people experienced. He himself was absolutely sure of escaping all that, buried as he was in his texts and his exercise books, cuirassed by his pride and armed by his ambition. And now, quite on the contrary, he liked this passage because he discerned in it the exact expression of his own state of mind.

For the moment, he felt soothed but in a few days, in an hour perhaps, sin would renew its attack, and the swirl of desires would once again sweep away his reason. His childhood was over. His youth was beginning and beginning against his will. How long would this ferment, this giddiness last for him? Would he have to abandon those plans for fame? Was his career going to be held up by five, by ten years possibly? Henceforth, an end to tranquillity. Without doubt, he would continue to come top of his class; he would stand out in his exams. But at the price of what struggles; amidst what agitation? If he had at least kept his faith, he would have had God as an ally in his tussle with his passions. But for a long time, religion was no more to him than the outdated ideal of a few pious old women.

Joanny invoked, not old age, but that time of life when once the turbulence of youth was spent, he could sit down again once and for all with his dictionaries and his papers in front of him — or with his life before him, which was more interesting than all the books ever written. A girl had just turned him down and he would have thanked her for it, had she restored him to his books and the elaboration of his great career. But she had returned him to her sister — her sisters, the family of women.

Oh, how weary he was! Life was insipid. He took no pleasure at all in thinking about his most recent first place. Fame itself was without interest. Encarnacion, the prettiest of the little Cuban girls — no, much better not to dwell on her. That was perhaps yet another disappointment he was storing up for himself. He followed his form to the dormitory, worn out, sickened, discontented with the world and himself, desiring nothing more than the oblivion of sleep.

He slept extremely badly and woke up only on the summons of the drum roll. All night, he had been dreaming that he was reciting a speech in Latin in the Archbishop's presence and it had seemed to him as though he were uttering, *ore rotundo*, an infinite number of fine endings and noble inflections: *abunt, arentur, ibus, arum* . . .

XVIII

And so Santos Iturria remained the untroubled master of his conquest. In a month's time, he was due to sit the papers of the second part of the baccalaureate in Paris and he had every chance of passing with distinction. Whilst his sixth-form friends spent their breaks cramming themselves with textbook formulas, Santos would stroll privately with Fermina Márquez in the grounds. Mama Doloré permitted these tête-à-têtes. She had always had a fondness for the Iturria brothers. And she had begun to cherish Santos most especially since that Whit Sunday when at the way out of the Spanish chapel in the Avenue Friedland, a very elegant young man had advanced to meet her, all smiles, and she had suddenly recognized the broad, handsome face of Santos, fresh and open, under a truly gleaming top hat. There was no gainsaying he was a real man; "and a man of the best society," the Creole lady would say.

She had nevertheless already seen him on two occasions in Paris; but it was at night-time and half dozing or inattentive, she had barely made him out. "Well, well, so you have managed to be given time off?" One evening at a late hour, he had come to the avenue Wagram to return to *La Chica* a bracelet she had dropped, that fool, while playing tennis in the grounds of Saint Augustine's. On another occasion, she and her nieces had met him quite by chance as they were leaving the Opéra Comique: he had difficulty in concealing the little uniform of the pupils from Saint Augustine's beneath a civilian overcoat. Mama Doloré was unable to follow any of this and all the less so since *La Chica* had implored her (but without caring to explain herself) never to speak of Mr Iturria to Saint Augustine's' prefect of studies.

But once she had seen Santos in broad daylight on the cobblestones of Paris and a Santos in frock coat, light-coloured gloves and fine shoes, she talked about him to everybody. It became her infatuation. She wrote specially to her brother in Columbia just to sing the praises of Santos Iturria. She went to make inquiries about the Iturria family at the Mexican legation. These particulars were satisfactory. Mama Doloré would consider *La Chica*. *Y cómo no?* Of course there was time: they were both still so young! And what did her niece think about it? That was the main point.

Yet it was not all that difficult to tell. Since Whitsun, *La Chica* was too gay and then too thoughtful. *La Chica* took an hour longer than she normally did to prepare herself on the days when they went to Saint Augustine's. *La Chica* was loved and perhaps in love.

At first, she was completely dejected: she thought she had reduced this poor Mr Léniot to despair. But was this her own fault? And besides, he was a child. Then she felt ashamed: "What must he be thinking of me?" She would have wished never to have trusted him with those secrets, never to have imparted those wholly pure thoughts from the time when she was still innocent and devout. "Hypocrite! He must be saying that I'm a hypocrite!" she would say to herself and, poisoned with remorse, she supposed that God was punishing her in this manner for her lack of self-constraint. She hardly had the courage to pray any more.

Yet the world ought to show understanding for our feelings instead of condemning us. At the very moment she had taken Joanny Léniot as the confidant for her religious ideas, she was beginning to struggle against this propensity which was drawing her towards human love. It was even to strengthen herself in her resistance to sin that she had sought these pious discussions, that she had said all those things which she had jealously guarded up until then. And her expectation had been disappointed. As she gave her religious fervour every freedom in expressing itself, so this fervour abandoned her. Without knowing it, this child had witnessed the death throes of her piety; it was the cry of this dying piety which he had heard. On returning one evening to her room, she had fallen sobbing to the carpet. She wanted to abase herself, to wipe away all the sin she could feel inside which was to overcome her. So she decided to lie stretched out facing the ceiling for one hour, with her feet joined together and her arms in the cross's form. But soon this was unbearable; oppressed, aching, the veins on her head swollen to bursting point, she could endure it no longer. She stood up again and looked at the face of her alarm clock: she had persevered for barely ten minutes. So she hurled herself passionately into what she called sin. She did not seek to excuse herself: she loved a man and that meant her soul was lost. She loved. And her night was so wonderful that she lived it in its entirety, that she drank in every dark minute of it with delight and only fell asleep at daybreak.

For her, this was the beginning of unforgettable nights. As she was absolutely incapable of closing her eyes, she wanted to spend every night reading and reading precisely those profane books which she had hitherto despised. She read in succession *Petitesses* by P. Luis Coloma, Jorge Isaacs' *Maria* and one or two of the Argentine novels by Carlos Maria Ocantos. But she was too preoccupied to give these authors a sustained attention. Her reading was a struggle with the pages: she would continuously slide the paper knife to the place she had reached in the book and, looking at the segment, she would compare the width of the pages she had already read to that of the pages she still had to read. Occasionally, however, she would forget herself enough to grasp the complete meaning of the phrases. Then she would become interested in the characters. Novels being something new for her, she did not see behind the narrative the literary devices, the commonplace, the age-old props which can be used anywhere and which end up by putting us off the defined past and all the novels of the world. She was like those members of an audience who have never seen the wings and who admire the scenery without reservations. She would begin to read as soon as she had returned to her room. She would lie down on her bed without taking off her evening gown in which she felt more beautiful and which she crumpled without caring. There was no doubting it, all the adventures of these characters really did not interest her; her own heart was too full of emotions; her own adventure was too wonderful. If the traitor had become Santos Iturria's friend, he would obviously have mended his ways and the final catastrophe would not have taken place. She pitied the Currita (in *Petitesses*); she felt sorry for all the black-hearted or unhappy heroines. They had never had the love of Santos Iturria to console or redeem them . . . She would close the book and think of her happiness. She would cast tender glances at the things surrounding her. The chandelier's electric lights, the illuminated bulbs of the wall lamps above the fireplace and on each side of the round mirror, all these lights shone pure and still, conveying a sense of security in the midst of this wealth. The walls hung in watered silk of old rose, the heavy and sumptuous furniture, the thick carpet covering the entire floor, the gold of the picture frames, the tables and pedestal stands inlaid with copper, the wardrobe, its three doors panelled with limpid mirrors, she would run a kindly eye over all these objects. A few weeks earlier, she detested them because they reminded her that the rich will not enter the Kingdom of Heaven, because they caused her anguish to think of all the poor wretches, of those who sleep in hostels, of those luckless souls who have fallen to society's depths and whose nakedness stands revealed to the very cores of their being. Now on the contrary, she liked them: this luxury was worthy of her heart's sovereign. As for her, she felt no attachment to it but wouldn't he be happy if he agreed to come and spend a few days at their home on the breaking up of his school where life was tough and frugal, yes wouldn't he be happy here? He would have the *feuille morte* bedroom which was even more opulent than this one and he would do his shopping in the victoria. Oh! If only that were possible!

She lowered her glance to her bare throat; she contemplated herself stretched out in her gorgeous dress, she admired the daintiness of her arched feet. Surely she too was worthy of her heart's sovereign? — The night hours have a romantic side. Two o'clock in the afternoon is prosaic, almost common; but two o'clock in the morning is an adventurer plunging into the unknown. And this unknown is three o'clock in the morning, the nocturnal pole, time's mysterious continent. You skirt round it and if you believe you have ever crossed it, you are mistaken for soon four o'clock arrives without your having discovered the secret of the night. And the dawn is already streaking the shutters with its parallel stripes of blue.

Now when Fermina Márquez appeared on the steps of the visiting room at Saint Augustine's, she had been up for barely two hours and there were rings under her wonderful eyes which would shut at the overvivid brightness of the sun. But her gait was nobler, more triumphant than ever. She would quite deliberately show herself before the pupils had left the refectory to provoke Santos, who having eaten his lunch in great haste and being obliged to stay at his bench, would stamp with impatience, ready to rush outside as soon as grace had been said.

How happy he seemed to us! We knew that he wore a lock of her hair wound round his right wrist and concealed beneath his cuff, which she had given to him, with the result that we did not shake his hand and brush his right arm without experiencing a feeling of respect: this lock rendered Santos' person sacred.

They used to stroll on the terrace. She had allowed him to smoke in her presence: his cigarette smoke had such a good, reassuring smell! She breathed it in with relish. She looked up

93

at him with an expression of solemnity and admiration. She was happy to be slightly less exalted than him. Everything he said affected her, made her joyful, caressed her.

Once or twice, they invited Demoisel to come and have tea with them in the grounds. We also saw them in the great avenue: they walked ahead of the group made up of Mama Doloré, Pilar and Paquito Márquez; Santos was on Fermina's left and Demoisel on her right. The Negro would stand absolutely straight and hold his head up high; he seemed very proud and very intimidated at the same time. From afar, you could see the whites of his eyes roll in his gleaming, black face. His manners were beyond reproach. He too was South American.

XIX

Ten days or so before prizegiving, as Joanny Léniot was standing in the playground, he heard his name being called by Santos Iturria.

"Mama Doloré has something to say to you; come."

He followed him. The whole family was on the terrace. He shook their hands. Mama Doloré enquired after his health, was charming. Joanny would have liked to have cut short the meeting. He was above all afraid of being left alone with Fermina. He was no longer so certain that he had not been ridiculous at their last encounter with his talk about his genius. He observed her surreptitiously. He was not surprised that she had discarded her ideas of humility and piety; that appeared natural to him: we outlive our emotions as we outlive the seasons. There was in her lovely frame a central, all-powerful force, of which her thoughts, desires and feelings were just passing modes. She was more beautiful than ever and seemed to have grown taller. He felt a mere child in her presence. He was not made to be loved by her; he ought never to have lost his heart to her.

He wanted to take his leave. But he was obliged to listen to Mama Doloré's word of thanks. "Mr Léniot, you showed my nephew so much kindness that I had no wish to demonstrate my gratitude in speech alone. So please accept this small something; may it remind you of us occasionally." She offered him a little package, a box wrapped up in tissue paper. Joanny reddened. His pride inclined him to refuse. He was on the point of doing so when Fermina Márquez passed close to him and murmured: "Accept." He obeyed her, made his thanks in a few words and withdrew.

It was only at the end of evening prep that he decided to open the box. It was a gold watch and chain; a thick, heavy chain. The face was in gold. His initials J.L. were engraved on the back. He felt a moment's gay surprise. The watch of Léniot senior was scarcely finer looking than this one. The box bore the name of a rue de la Paix jeweller. Mama Doloré must easily have had to pay five or six hundred francs for it. So the Creole lady cared a lot for him? Why then hadn't she said: "Until our next meeting"? He remembered her words: "You showed my nephew so much kindness . . . " So that was it. "But then," thought Joanny suddenly, "but then they paid me off!" Yes, of course that was it. This present was not a token of affection, a present that is made to a family friend. It was the settlement of a service rendered: it was made at the end, at the moment when relations were being brought to a close.

"They paid me off!" Joanny succumbed beneath the insult. "They paid me off!" His cheeks had turned red all of a sudden and the flush remained like the visible mark of a slap, painful as a burn. "They paid me off!" Yes, they wished to owe him nothing; they had dismissed him by generously paying him his wages. Oh! The wretches! Oh! The wretches! And it was with smiles that they destroyed my dignity. That was the way of the rich: they used their money to hurt those they despised. Joanny looked at all his companions, his eyes dry and burning. And he realized that he hated them because they were wealthy. Until that moment, he had not been aware of this. Those two hundred thousand francs his father earned each year from the silk trade brought him the respect and greetings of the folk in his neighbourhood and made his family the potentates of its village in the department of the Loire. Even in Lyons, Léniot senior was a grandee and Joanny, as the only son, had his share of that fame. But what was that compared to the wealth of all these sons of nabobs, to the millions these South Americans had which their fathers sent to Europe aboard ships which belonged to them?

"They paid me off!" His hands clenching his desk, Joanny eyed the prep group, livid with rage. How calm they all were, huddled like this over their exercise books, these sons of kings! "They paid me off!" It was the supreme insult. The poor at least, even if they were striking you, made an effort, grimaced. The rich remained sitting down, spoke to you softly and destroyed you. All his friends' parents would have acted in the same manner. "For those people I am a beggar and they look down on me. They have the gall to despise me who am so intellectually superior to all of them!"

"They paid me off! . . ." Joanny remembered an incident in his childhood. One day, his parents had said to one of their workmen: "Please bring your son to spend the afternoons here; he will keep Mr Joanny company." At the end of eight days, the urchin had been returned to his father because he had already taught Mr Joanny lewd expressions. And the workman had been given a present to "pay for the hire of the young lout," Léniot senior had said. Joanny asked for permission to leave prep. He was holding the watch and chain in his closed fist.

At the end of a passage there was an abandoned classroom, next to the detention room. Its door had been boarded up; its window, which overlooked a small yard bounded by the main building and the wall of the riding school, had been blocked up by means of boards nailed to the frame; and higher up, a gap had been sealed off with tar paper. Pupils had amused themselves by piercing this paper with stones. They took pleasure in hearing the reverberation of their missiles as they dropped into this unknown place, on to this floor (or on to those benches?) they had never seen. Many dilapidated things could always be got rid of in this way: pen holders, broken rulers, used-up toiletries. The dreamiest of the younger ones, little Camille Moûtier for example, could not imagine the appearance of this lifeless chamber without trembling. And the proximity of the detention room, where we were confined only in the most serious of cases, was all that was necessary to make it a sacred place, consecrated to the fearsome gods.

Léniot leant with his back against the wall of the riding school, took deliberate aim and with a sudden movement, sent the watch and chain flying through the perforated paper. He heard two sounds: the object must first have hit the wall at the far end of the room and then come down on the wooden floor. – He returned to prep, relieved.

The next day on waking up, an idea occurred to him: wouldn't Mama Doloré be surprised not to receive a letter from his parents thanking her for their son's present? Because of course he would never speak of this matter to his parents. And he could already hear Mama Doloré saying to her niece: "Those Léniots haven't even sent me a note of thanks; those people don't know how to live." And her niece would remember what Joanny Léniot had said in her presence: "Tradesmen, financiers, every sort and kind of common person."

And on prizegiving day (they would certainly come to it), they would be astonished not to see the heavy, fine-looking watch chain on his waistcoat. And were his parents also to come from Lyons to witness his scholastic triumph, they would barely acknowledge the Márquezes about whom he had never said anything to them in his letters. Ah! What a blunder his pride had made him commit. But it was almost stealing! We are without question entitled to take pleasure in the things we are given but we have no right to destroy them; that is truly to wrong the giver. It would have been better not to accept.

No indeed! It would definitely have been better to keep those trinkets. If only to have a physical memento of Fermina Márquez. After all, this watch was not lost. If the prefect of studies were informed that an object as valuable as that could be found in this room, he would not hesitate to have the door broken down. But to notify him of this, Joanny would have to admit the truth. And he could never summon up the courage to do so.

He had fallen out with the Márquezes. He would not see them again. So much the better. He would not seek to make connections like Julien Morot! And as for her, well what of it? It was over! He had been stupid and ridiculous in her presence. It was therefore better that he no longer saw her, that she did not come to remind him any more that he had been stupid and ridiculous at an altogether forgettable moment in his life. And he most certainly had been. It still made him blush. Ah! That seduction plan and all that infantile talk!

For several days, he remained in the depths of despair, wallowing in the reeking swamps of self-contempt. He pulled himself out of this by reflecting with pride: "Here am I, Léniot, with so many grounds to be pleased with myself, filled with self-loathing." He marvelled at his modesty; the contrast created by the apparent good fortune of his destiny and the melancholy of his nature. He compared himself to a king covered in glory and yet weary of life. In a week's time, it would be prizegiving, his wonderful day of triumph, all red and golden. Joanny would be dazed by the applause greeting his name, repeated twenty times by the announcer of the list of prize winners. And despite that, he would take a sombreness of mind and lugubrious thoughts to the rostrum. But no, since this idea afforded him pleasure, his self-satisfaction was restored.

Without lessons to learn, prepared work to do, punishments to fear, the last days of the school year have arrived. They are so marvellous that you no longer remember what you have done with them. I firmly believe they were like great, empty rooms wholly bathed in sunlight: yes, thanks to there being none of the usual lessons and homework, they resembled reception rooms out of which all the furniture has been taken so that there can be dancing. It was the period when I would

99

take stock of my year, congratulating myself for not having merited a single punishment, for I too was an excellent pupil. And I was pleased because I was going to receive, as one might a superb, gold ingot, my form's prize for excellence. It was an important landmark in my life, this prize for excellence: thanks to it, you were certain of having done very well; with it, you did not need to look any higher; you had *made it*. To think that I would never again have the prize for excellence!

Joanny was already too old to reread the novels in the series *School Life by Country*; but he knew that these last days can be profitably employed by reading with care *The Ancient City* by Fustel de Coulanges or alternatively Gaston Boissier's master-piece *Cicero and his Friends*. Meanwhile, he would leaf through his corrected exercise books; the subject of each piece of homework was the memory of a triumph for him. In one of these exercise books, on a flyleaf, he had written down two letters: F.M.; and beneath, a date; the date of the bait on that famous evening when he had taken the decision to seduce a certain girl. He pondered for a moment. Then with a frightening seriousness, above the initials and the date, he set down this phrase taken from the *Commentaries on the Gallic Wars*: "*Hoc unum ad pristinam fortunam Caesari defuit.*"

XX

Since I left Saint Augustine's, taking away my last prize for excellence under my arm, I have visited our dear old school on two occasions. My first visit took place in the spring of 1902, several years after the institution had closed for good; and the second was more recently when I had written a large part of this tale. Saint Augustine's had just been expropriated for I don't know what reason, and it could not be entered without the administration's special authorization.

"It's not even worth the trouble to go and ask them for it, they don't grant it to anybody," the caretaker told me through a narrow grille built into the main door.

So I had to content myself with a look at the outer walls and, from the tramway platform, the tops of the trees in the grounds towards Bagneux. A few minutes later, I found myself on the place du Théâtre-Français, which was practically deserted because it was Sunday morning. This visit had barely taken me more than an hour. My childhood and youth strike me as being already so far away as in reality they are near to the place du Théâtre-Français which I go past almost every day.

It is of my first visit in 1902 that I wish to speak at length.

At first sight, you could not tell that anything had changed. The entrance was that same bare hall, with a great, black cross nailed up in the middle of the yellowish wall. And on the right was the caretaker's lodge with a grille and a high, openwork barrier. And in the lodge was the same caretaker as in our day, grown a little old — notably his imperial which had turned grey; and his decorations, instead of being spread out on his blue livery dolman with its silver buttons, were condensed into one single but enormous rosette which adorned the buttonhole of his rather ordinary jacket. He undoubtedly missed the sumptuous and sober livery of Saint Augustine's.

He recognized me almost at once and greeted me gaily with an oath in Spanish.

"Forgive me, sir; but I am so pleased when I see one of my old pupils again. And really all of you are my pupils a little bit: I brought you up. You were so small when you were sent here. You French boys, that was one thing; but I don't understand those South Americans who used to send their children here at such a young age with half the world separating them. Those poor abandoned mites. I've fought in wars, sir; I'm a hard man; well sometimes I've wept, yes wept, seeing them unable to get used to this place. And as for those who used to die! The Negroes, you know. More died in that sick bay than you were told about. "Their parents have taken them away," was the way they used to explain it. Sure, their parents took them away in a box . . . That poor little fellow who was so good at his work and so gentle, Delavache from Haiti, well, he died in my arms upstairs; that's the truth. Ah! When I think back on it! . . .

"Sure there were some amongst them who were not up to much; madcaps who would do things which shouldn't be done. But the folk from those tropical countries, they're like the natives in the colonies; they're precocious, too warm blooded. But what the heck! Most of them were in good health and kind hearted, real gentlemen who respected the good Lord and had no fear of anything. Yes, for a fine generation, that's all I need say.

"Look, let's go and sit on the steps of the visiting room. I've put a bench there and that's where I smoke my pipe after lunch. You've got the time, haven't you?

"When the school was sold, as somebody was required to look after the buildings and the grounds, I was appointed the caretaker with a small salary. I could've found a more lucrative post. But I know nobody any more. And I was set in my ways here. I like the open air; I could never get used to those flats in Paris, they're so small. Remember I have the whole of these grounds to walk about in . . .

"And so you said to yourself, just like that: 'That's an idea, I'll go and take a stroll round Saint Augustine's; that was kind of you. I felt sure you'd come back some day. I still see quite a few old pupils. It's easy for those living in Paris to come. Through them, I get news of the others. Many have died, sir, many have died. Some of them were just too rich, you see; that was their undoing. No sooner were they let out than they started to live it up. Those foul women are capable of anything. Besides, you have only to see where they come from; anyway, try as you will, what's bred in the bone will out in the flesh. Some lost everything gambling or on the stockmarket and killed themselves; others quite simply caroused to their deaths. What can one do? Well, too bad for them: you reap what you sow. What's sad is the death of that poor, little chap who was so clever, Léniot, Léniot (Joanny). You didn't know about it? It was his poor father who told me about it in tears, on this very spot. Well here it is: he died in his barracks during an epidemic four months after he was enlisted. Those garrisons in the east are tough for recruits, above all the blockhouses. Anyway he has died. A young chap who had started out so well. It appears that he had already obtained two degrees and a prize at the Faculty of Law in Paris before he was twenty-one.

I also get occasional visits from South America. They come to spend a year with us in Europe. So Marti minor is in Paris at this moment. He came to see me a fortnight or eighteen days ago. Mr Montemayor from Valparaiso, I saw him as well; about a year ago now. He brought along one of his brothers whom I didn't know, who wasn't raised here . . . It's strange about those South Americans: of two brothers (it's an observation I've often made), of two brothers, the elder one is always more — how should I put it? — more European: a pink-and-white complexion, chestnut hair and sometimes blue eyes as well; in a word, you would swear he was a Frenchman. The younger one, by contrast, has a dark colouring and the hair of a black man! In short, he's a real Indian. You know, just like the two Iturrias; do you remember them well?

"And now that I think about it, he came too, Iturria major. Santos, as you all used to call him. He came, hang on, two years ago in 1900; of course, the year of the Fair. He even spent two afternoons with me here. The first time he brought his wife. A lovely-looking person he married, Mr Iturria (Santos), a blonde lady, a German I think. Because after leaving Saint Augustine's, the two Iturria boys went to study in Germany . . . A lovely-looking person, my word! And the two of them together made a handsome couple . . . He told me that their father had become minister of war in their country, in Mexico. That doesn't surprise me: they were such fine people, those Iturrias, and so intelligent! We need men like that today in France. It's not that there aren't any. But people no longer pay any attention to merit; it's money that determines everything these days. So you can be honest or not as you like, seeing that you have the readies . . . What you used to learn in this school of Saint Augustine was precisely not to attach any importance to money. For us, it was just a means to succeed in turning out a decent person. That was why you were brought up the hard way. And there was even too much strictness; they could easily have let you come and go as you pleased in these grounds. It's true you wouldn't really be put off going there for a smoke without permission, you and your gang of old daredevils! . . . You know when all's said and done, there's nothing like discipline to form men and real men like those of my day. All those bourgeois nowadays look like workers who have won first prize in the lottery and think only of pampering themselves . . . "

I listened to the old boy fairly absent-mindedly. I looked at the playground before us. It was nothing more than a field of tall grasses, whose long, delicate tips swayed in the wind. Slender stalks had grown in between the pebbles, those pretty, smooth pebbles of the Seine valley, all veined with delightful colours. Beyond, the grounds drew my gaze; doubtless, nature had blurred their outline; but to what extent? I would have liked to go and see straight away. "Well now, sir, I can see that I've bored you enough with my chatter. I'll leave you to look round on your own: it's better: I would get in the way. Everything is open and you can stay for as long as you like. When you leave, I'll be in my lodge."

I rather took to the sentimental tone of the old soldier. He understood what a visit to the school meant to one of *his* old pupils; and the elegiac turn to his words was not wholly unintentional. Above all, I admired the delicacy of feeling conveyed at the end: "I would get in the way."

And in truth, I had really no idea where to start my visit. I saw everything higgeldy-piggeldy, without method, endlessly retracing my steps. The stones of the terrace's central staircase were loose. The branches of the mighty trees which had no longer been pruned for years, grew in every direction. Grass overran the avenues. In front of the visiting room, purslane, which doubtless had broken out of the large orange-tree pots where it had been planted, crept and bloomed between the paving stones.

I sat down in my old place at prep. What a fantastic thing time is! Nothing had changed; there was a little more dust on the desks; that was all. And here was I, grown to manhood. If, by dint of listening to this silence, I were suddenly to make out a faraway murmuring of both voices and footsteps beyond the passage of the years . . . And if all the pupils of my day were suddenly to come back into this prep room and if, waking to the noise, I were to find myself facing my texts and schoolboy exercise books again . . . "Many have died, sir, many have died."

I returned to the grounds, to the sunshine. The village lads had succeeded in smashing a few of the chapel's stained-glass windows with stones. The house in which the prefect of studies used to live was completely ruined. The statue of Saint Augustine on the terrace had almost entirely lost its gilt. I took a long time to rediscover the site where the tennis court had been installed in Fermina Márquez' day — I had to go through a thicket which certainly used not to exist then. I caught myself saying out loud: "What about Fermina Márquez?" Yes, what had happened to her? I presumed she was married now! And I liked to think she was happy.

I went back to the terrace. Over yonder lay Paris where I would be in a little while, so removed from all that. Above me, the birds made their innocent voices heard; indifferent to the changes of regime, they continued to celebrate the glory of the kingdom of France from one summer to the next and perhaps, like the caretaker, to extol the education we received at the school of Saint Augustine as well.

Over the visiting room — the Louis XV part of the buildings — I saw a bull's eye window with all its sumptuous mouldings stained by the rain. The panes had been broken, the frame pulled out and so it stayed, wide open to today's sunshine, to the sky's blue: this Parisian sky, so astir with activity, with mists, vapours, halo of lights, balloons and Sundays. The bull's eye no longer reflected anything of all that! The bull's eye was pierced on the outside of the deserted attics which nobody went to see any more.

What else was missing in this inventory of fixtures? Ah! Yes: on the wall of the main courtyard, the marble plaque on which were engraved the names of the

PUPILS WHO DIED FOR THEIR COUNTRY
AND THEIR FAITH

was cracked.

QUARTET ENCOUNTERS

The purpose of this paperback series is to bring together influential and outstanding works of twentieth-century European literature in translation. Each title has an introduction by a distinguished contemporary writer, describing a personal or cultural 'encounter' with the text, as well as placing it within its literary and historical perspective.

Quartet Encounters will concentrate on fiction, although the overall emphasis is upon works of enduring literary merit, whether biography, travel, history or politics. The series will also preserve a balance between new and older works, between new translations and reprints of notable existing translations. Quartet Encounters provides a much-needed forum for prose translation, and makes accessible to a wide readership some of the more unjustly neglected classics of modern European literature.

Aharon Appelfeld · *The Retreat*

'A small masterpiece . . . the vision of a remarkable poet'
New York Times Book Review

Alain · *The Gods*

'There are not a few of us in the world who think Alain was, and remains, one of the greatest men of our time. I would not myself hesitate to say, the greatest'
André Maurois

Gaston Bachelard · *The Psychoanalysis of Fire*

'. . . he is a philosopher, with a professional training in
the sciences, who devoted most of the second phase of
his career to promoting that aspect of human nature
which often seems most inimical to science: the poetic
imagination . . .'
J.G. Weightman, *The New York Review of Books*

Robert Bresson · *Notes on the Cinematographer*

'[Bresson] is the French cinema, as Dostoyevsky
is the Russian novel and Mozart is German music'
Jean-Luc Godard, *Cahiers du Cinéma*

Hermann Broch · *The Sleepwalkers*

'One of the greatest European novels . . .
masterful' Milan Kundera

E.M. Cioran · *The Temptation to Exist*

'Cioran is one of the most delicate minds of real power
writing today. Nuance, irony, and refinement are the
essence of his thinking . . .' Susan Sontag

Stig Dagerman · *The Games of Night*

'One is haunted by a secret and uneasy suspicion
that [Dagerman's] private vision, like Strindberg's
and Kafka's, may in fact be nearer the truth of things
than those visions of the great humanists, such as
Tolstoy and Balzac, which people call universal'
Michael Meyer

Stig Dagerman · *German Autumn*

'[German Autumn] attracted, and still deserves,
attention, partly because [Dagerman] had a sharp eye for
concrete details, partly because he could argue
pungently, but mainly because he dared to see German

individuals as suffering human beings rather than simply as tokens of national disgrace or guilt' Robin Fulton

Grazia Deledda · *After the Divorce*

'What [Deledda] does is create the passionate complex of a primitive populace' D.H. Lawrence

Marcellus Emants · *A Posthumous Confession*

'Since the time of Rousseau we have seen the growth of the genre of the *confessional novel*, of which *A Posthumous Confession* is a singularly pure example. Termeer [the narrator], claiming to be unable to keep his dreadful secret, records his confession and leaves it behind as a monument to himself, thereby turning a worthless life into art' J.M. Coetzee

Carlo Emilio Gadda · *That Awful Mess on Via Merulana*

'One of the greatest and most original Italian novels of our time' Alberto Moravia

Andrea Giovene · *Sansevero*

'Some novels can be flirted with, others constitute a brief affair. Occasionally one is lured into a long marriage, when the early tensions and subsequent *longueurs* stabilize at last into a solid relationship. So it is reading *The Book of Giuliano Sansevero*. One can see why, on its way to this country . . . its author has been compared with Proust and Lampedusa' *Daily Telegraph*

Martin A. Hansen · *The Liar*

'[The Liar] is both a vindication of religious truth and a farewell to the traditional modes of extended fiction. It is haunted by literary ghosts, and English readers will recognize the shadowy forms of Hans Anderson . . . and Søren Kierkegaard' Eric Christiansen

Eugene Ionesco · *Fragments of a Journal*

'I am not too sure whether I am dreaming or remembering, whether I have lived or dreamt it. Memories quite as much as dreams arouse in me the strongest feelings of the unreality and the ephemerality of the world . . .'
Eugene Ionesco, *Present Past, Past Present*

Gustav Janouch · *Conversations with Kafka*

'I read it and was stunned by the wealth of new material . . . which plainly and unmistakably bore the stamp of Kafka's genius' Max Brod

Ismaïl Kadaré · *The General of the Dead Army*

'Ismaïl Kadaré is presenting his readers not merely with a novel of world stature — which is already a great deal — but also, and even more important, with a novel that is the voice of ancient Albania herself, speaking to today's world of her rebirth' Robert Escarpit

Miroslav Krleža · *On the Edge of Reason*

'Paris had its Balzac and Zola; Dublin, its Joyce; Croatia, its Krleža . . . one of the most accomplished, profound authors in European literature . . .'
Saturday Review

Pär Lagerkvist · *The Dwarf*

'A considerable imaginative feat'
Times Literary Supplement

Valery Larbaud · *Fermina Marquez*

'As a psychological study of male adolescence it is delicate, touching, unsentimental; the atmosphere of the school is evoked with an unforgettable nostalgic vivacity' Francis Wyndham

Osip Mandelstam · *The Noise of Time*

'Clarence Brown's translation of Mandelstam not only gives English readers the greatest twentieth-century stylist in Russian but is also one of the finest examples ever of the translator's art: a miracle of accuracy, tone and feeling of period' Guy Davenport

Henry de Montherlant · *The Bachelors*

'One of those carefully framed, precise and acid studies on a small canvas in which French writers again and again excel' V.S. Pritchett

Stratis Myrivilis · *Life in the Tomb*

'*Life in the Tomb* has moments of great literary beauty and of more than one kind of literary power. In 1917, Myrivilis was twenty-five. "Before I entered the trenches I had not the slightest inkling of life's true worth. From now on, however, I shall savour its moments one by one . . ." ' Peter Levi

Pier Paolo Pasolini · *A Dream of Something*

'. . . indisputably the most remarkable figure to have emerged in Italian arts and letters since the Second World War' Susan Sontag

Luigi Pirandello · *Short Stories*

'The outer world of Pirandello's stories – the appearance of its reality – has a deceptive monotony and a deceptive variety. The monotony is the mask which society exacts from us; the variety is the pathetic series of fragmentary masks in which we strut about the world' Frederick May

D.R. Popescu · *The Royal Hunt*

'Popescu's style may be compared to that of Gabriel García Márquez in *One Hundred Years of Solitude*, although it is more concrete and somewhat sharper . . .'
J.E. Cottrell and M. Bogdan

Rainer Maria Rilke · *Rodin and other Prose Pieces*

'[Rilke's] essay remains the outstanding interpretation of Rodin's œuvre, anticipating and rendering otiose almost all subsequent criticism'
William Tucker, *The Language of Sculpture*

Rainer Maria Rilke · *Selected Letters 1902–1926*

'By will-power and concentration, a sense of which is immanent in all his letters, as if some great quiet animal were crouching there, Rilke made himself into a great European genius, probably the last of the breed' John Bayley

Lou Andreas-Salomé · *The Freud Journal*

'Lou Andreas-Salomé was a woman with a remarkable flair for great men and . . . it was said of her that she had attached herself to the greatest men of the nineteenth and twentieth centuries Nietzsche and Freud respectively'
Ernest Jones, *The Life and Work of Sigmund Freud*

Stanislaw Ignacy Witkiewicz · *Insatiability*

'A study of decay: mad, dissonant music, erotic perversion, . . . and complex psychopathic personalities'
Czeslaw Milosz